0

RUN

Also by Kody Keplinger

The DUFF
Lying Out Loud
A Midsummer's Nightmare
Shut Out

KODY KEPLINGER

RUN

Hodder
Children's
Books

HODDER CHILDREN'S BOOKS

First published in the United States by Scholastic Inc.

First published in Great Britain in 2016 by Hodder Children's Books

3 5 7 9 10 8 6 4 2

A CIP catalogue record for this book is available from the British Library

ISBN: 978 1 444 93270 6

Typeset in Berkeley by Avon DataSet Ltd, Bidford-on-Avon, Warwickshire

Printed and bound in Great Britain by Clays Ltd, St Ives plc

The paper and board used in this book are from well-managed forests
and other responsible sources.

Hodder Children's Books
An imprint of Hachette Children's Group
Part of Hodder & Stoughton
Carmelite House
50 Victoria Embankment
London EC4Y 0DZ

An Hachette UK Company
www.hachette.co.uk

For Shana
Because there's no one else I could
dedicate this story to.
I love you.

BO

I'm waiting for the sirens.

I know it don't make much sense. The police ain't coming for me – not yet, anyway – but I already feel like a fugitive.

My flip-flops slap against the muddy ground, and soggy leaves cling to my bare legs. Tree limbs catch and tangle and snap in my hair. I should've put it up before I left. But I'd barely had time to pack, let alone think about my damn hair.

'Slow down, stupid dog.' Utah's leash cuts into my fingers. She's running faster than I can, her tail swishing back and forth, like this is some kinda game.

By the time we reach the edge of the woods, I'm panting harder than the dog is. My chest hurts and my lungs feel like they're screaming for air, but I ain't got time to catch my breath.

She's waiting for me, standing there behind her parents' garage. In the moonlight, she looks like some sorta ghost. Her skin is so white it seems to glow, and her long black hair is darker than the night around her. She looks beautiful, and I look feral. Not that she can see me or anything else right now.

'Agnes,' I whisper, so as not to scare her. My voice is ragged. I swallow and say her name again. 'Agnes.'

'Bo?'

'Right here.'

I'm about to reach out for her when Utah decides she's got first dibs. Agnes squeals, startled, as my dog jumps up and licks her right on the nose.

'Shh!' I yank Utah back, and Agnes covers her mouth.

Neither of us move for a minute. We stand, frozen, listening. But the only sounds are the crickets and a few loudmouthed bullfrogs down by the Putnams' pond.

Slowly, Agnes lowers her hand. 'You brought the dog? Really, Bo?'

'Sure as hell ain't gonna leave her,' I say. 'Did you get the keys?'

She nods and reaches into the front pocket of her jeans. She holds them out about a foot to my left. I don't say nothing, though. I take a quick step to the side and

2

wrap my hand around two cold keys, their jagged edges digging into my palm.

'Come on.' I take her arm and loop it through mine, then guide her around the side of the detached garage. Utah trots along on my left, while Agnes's cane makes quiet thuds in the grass to my right. 'Which key?' I ask when we get to the side door.

'Neither. They never lock the garage.'

'They're crazy.'

'Nothing's been stolen before.'

'Until now.'

'I'm not sure this counts as stealing.'

But I'm pretty damn sure it does.

I turn the knob and push open the door. Agnes lets go of my arm and slides her hand along the wall until she finds the light switch. A fluorescent light flickers on above us, revealing two cars parked side by side. One is the Atwoods' regular car, a white Toyota. But the other is an old silver Chevy I ain't seen before.

'My sister's car,' Agnes says, like she's reading my mind. 'She's still at college, so nobody's using it.'

'Won't she be home for summer soon, though?'

Agnes shrugs. 'We need it more than she does.'

I can't argue with that. Agnes and I toss our stuff in the back. Neither of our bags are heavy. We just packed what we absolutely needed. 'Hop in, Utah,' I say, patting the backseat. She climbs in and licks the side of my face before I shut the door.

Agnes gets into the passenger's seat, and I run to turn off the garage light before I slide behind the wheel. Above my head, attached to the visor, is an automatic garage door opener.

'Will your parents hear?'

'No,' Agnes says. 'They sleep like rocks.'

My heart is pounding and my hands are slick with sweat as I shove one of the keys into the ignition. It takes me a few tries to get it to turn over, and the revving is so loud it makes me flinch. Her parents had better sleep like the dead, or else we ain't even getting out of the driveway. The clock on the dash-board lights up and tells me it's just past 3:00 a.m.

'Agnes,' I say, choking on her name. 'You sure you wanna do this?'

'No.' She turns her head, and this time she's looking right at me. 'But I'm doing it anyway.'

I almost start to cry, right then and there, but I blink back the tears. My fingers fumble with the garage door opener, and a second later the groaning and creaking starts. I watch the gap between the door and ground get wider and wider. It's been open a good minute before

I shift the car into gear, and Agnes's hand reaches out to cover mine.

'Love you, Bo,' she says.

'Love you, too.'

AGNES

Every small town has that family. You hear their last name and you just shake your head because you know the whole lot of them are trouble. Not one will make it to their twenty-first birthday without being arrested at least once. Maybe it's in their blood, or maybe it's just how they're raised. It's hard to say. All you can do is steer clear because nothing good can come of getting mixed up with that bunch.

In Mursey, that family was the Dickinsons.

'They're no good,' I grew up hearing my grandmother say every time we'd pass the double-wide where a few of them lived, on our way to church. 'They're dirty drunks and thieves. And godless, too. None of them have stepped foot in a church in generations. Probably get struck by lightning if they did.'

'Mama, please,' Daddy would say. 'Don't fill Agnes's

6

head with all that. There's a Dickinson girl in her class.'

'That's why she ought to find out now,' Grandma said. 'Don't want her getting too friendly with that girl. She'll grow up just like the rest of them, and I don't want Agnes to be dragged down with her.'

My parents did their best to teach me the Golden Rule – treating others the way you want to be treated and all – but it was hard to argue with Grandma when the whole town seemed to agree. The Dickinsons were a bad lot; it was a reputation they'd earned nearly a hundred years back, if town legend was correct, and it was a reputation they wouldn't be shaking anytime soon.

You couldn't miss a Dickinson, either. They all had lots of wavy strawberry-blond hair and eyes the colour of sweet tea. At least, that's what I'd been told. I wasn't able to make out the colour of their eyes or anybody else's. Those little details escaped my vision. I'd been told most of the family had freckles, too, but that was something else I'd just have to take everyone's word for.

Bo Dickinson looked just like the rest of the family. Her hair – the one feature I could really notice – was a wavy mane of gold with hints of red. Sometimes she wore it in a sloppy ponytail, but most of the time it was loose and unkempt, a mess of tangled curls and unbrushed waves. Seemed fitting, really. Her hair was as wild as she was.

Assuming the stories were right, that is. We were in the same grade, though I'd never spoken more than two words to her. But if even half the gossip was true, Bo Dickinson was wild.

'She's a slut, that's what she is.'

'Christy,' I hissed.

We were standing on the front steps of the Mursey Baptist Church, where we met every week before Sunday school. The minute I'd arrived this morning, Christy had grabbed my arm, pulled me aside, and said, 'You won't believe what Bo Dickinson did.' But five minutes had passed, and Christy still hadn't gotten to whatever Bo had done. Instead, she'd spent the time recapping a whole bunch of old gossip, just in case I'd forgotten.

Bo Dickinson's life was like a novel the whole town was working on. A collaboration that had been going on for sixteen years. You couldn't start a new chapter without looking back on what had been written before.

'It just feels wrong,' I said. 'Saying the word *slut* in church.'

'Why? God thinks she's a slut, too. And besides, we're not in the church yet. And I haven't even gotten to what she did Friday night.'

'All right, well, what?'

8

Christy gripped my arm and squeezed. It was a thing she always did when she was excited about something. Or mad about something. 'Sarah told me she heard Perry Schaffer telling his friends that Bo' – she leaned in closer and lowered her voice – 'that Bo went down on him in the hayloft at Andrew's party Friday night.'

'Doesn't Perry have a girlfriend?'

'Yeah. Layla Masters. And she was at the party, too. I saw her.'

'Wait . . . You went to Andrew's party Friday?'

Andrew was her on-and-off-again boyfriend. And as of Friday morning, at school, they'd been off.

Christy took a step back and adjusted her short auburn ponytail. 'Yeah. Sorry, Agnes. I would have taken you with me, but Andrew wanted to talk, and I knew it would be too dark in his barn for you to see real well. I didn't want to be guiding you around all night. You understand, right?'

'Sure.'

'And Andrew and I worked things out.'

'That's good.'

'But Bo! Can you believe it? Something is wrong with that girl.'

I nodded.

'And Layla is gonna freak out. I bet they'll get in a

fight in the cafeteria. Hair pulling and everything.'

'You'd like that, wouldn't you.'

I didn't know the voice at first. I hadn't heard it enough to connect a person with it. That's how I recognized people most of the time. Faces were just a jumble of blurred features to me, but everyone had a different voice. A different rhythm to their speech. If I knew a voice well enough, I could pick it out of a crowd, just like everybody else spotted a face.

Not this voice, though. It hadn't imprinted itself on my brain. Not yet.

Christy and I both turned, and I could see someone standing at the bottom of the church steps. For once, my vision was enough. The bright late-August sun glinted off a mane of thick, wavy hair. It was gold and red. A halo with a hint of hellfire.

Bo Dickinson.

My stomach clenched, and my fist tightened around my cane. Part of me expected her to lunge at us. For our hair to be pulled. Or our eyes clawed out. I'd never been in a fight before, and Christy hadn't, either – as far as I knew – but I was sure Bo Dickinson had. And my guess was, she was the type to fight mean and dirty.

If Christy was scared, I couldn't tell. She put on her

Sunday school voice and said, 'Good morning, Bo. You joining us for church today?'

Bo didn't say anything. For a second, she just stood there. I didn't know, but I guessed she was probably staring me and Christy down. My heart had lodged itself in my throat, and I wasn't too sure if I'd ever breathe normally again.

But then, to my surprise, the burning halo began to move away, down the sidewalk.

'Maybe next week?' Christy hollered after her. 'Jesus loves you, Bo.' Then, under her breath, she murmured, 'Whore. Probably on a walk of shame home right now. No other reason to be out this early on a Sunday unless you're church-bound.'

'Christy, Agnes,' Brother Thomas called from the top of the steps. 'It's almost nine, girls. Y'all come on inside and head to your class.'

'Coming, sir,' Christy said. 'You ready, Agnes?'

I stared down the street, my eyes following the back of Bo's head until she was too far away and the golden-red colours blurred with the rest of the hazy world around me.

'Agnes!' Christy tugged on my free hand. 'Come on.'

'Oh, sorry.' I turned around and followed her into the church, my cane tapping the corner of each step.

'Can you believe that?' I whispered as we made our way across the sanctuary and toward the hallway that led to the classrooms.

'What?'

'Bo,' I said. 'That she just walked away.'

'Of course she did,' Christy said. 'What was she gonna do, beat us up right in front of Brother Thomas? Besides, even Bo would never hit a blind girl.'

My sister hadn't gone to church with us that day. Actually, she hadn't been to church with us in a while. Not since she turned eighteen and declared that Mama and Daddy couldn't make her go anymore. They'd tried. And Grandma had called and given her a talking-to. But Gracie didn't budge.

Most of the time, she'd sleep in on Sunday morning and was gone when the rest of us got home. I was never sure where she went all day. There was hardly anything to do in Mursey on Sundays, and most of her friends had to be in church. The whole town was in church. Except the Dickinsons, but I doubted Gracie was hanging out with them.

Mama and Daddy didn't question her much, though. Not lately. She was less than a week from leaving for college in Lexington, and she was spending as much

12

of that time out of the house as she could.

She still hadn't gotten home by the time I went to bed that night, but my parents had left the porch light on for her.

'She's an adult now,' Mama said. 'She can stay out a little late if she wants.'

It was just past one in the morning when I got up to use the bathroom. I had to hold my alarm clock up to my face to read the red numbers. I climbed out of bed and crept through the house in the dark, sliding my hand along the walls. I didn't need my cane or any lights on. We'd lived in this house since I was born, and I knew it as well as I knew the sound of my mother's voice. I could probably have left for years, not step foot in this house for decades, only to come back and still be able to find my way around in the dark without a second thought.

Not that that was real likely. Best I could figure, I'd probably grow old in this house.

The bathroom was right at the top of the stairs. I looked down and saw that the lamp in the living room was still on, which meant Gracie wasn't back yet. She always turned it off on her way up to bed. With the light on, I could make out some of the living room furniture – the back of Daddy's recliner, the coffee table, one side of the tan couch. It was still blurry, and if it had been anyone else's house, I wouldn't have been able to tell what a bit of it was. But it was my living room; it hadn't changed in years, so my memory filled in some of the gaps my eyes couldn't.

I opened the bathroom door, not bothering to turn on the light. There was no point unless I was checking my reflection, and I sure didn't want to do that. Even I could see how messy my hair got after a few hours of sleep.

I'd just finished washing my hands and shut off the tap when I heard the front door open downstairs. I poked my head out of the bathroom and watched as shadows crossed the living room.

'Come on,' my sister's voice whispered.

'What about your parents?'

I didn't know that voice, but it belonged to a boy.

'They're heavy sleepers,' Gracie told him. 'And we'll sneak you out before they get up in the morning.'

'You sure?'

'You don't want to?'

'No. Believe me, I do.'

The shadows weren't crisp enough for me to make out what they were doing, but I knew what it sounded like when people kissed. Not from personal experience – just TV and some awkward encounters in the hallways at school – but that's what my sister and this boy were doing at the bottom of the stairs.

I felt my cheeks heat up.

After a second, the kissing sounds stopped. Gracie giggled. 'Let's go upstairs,' she whispered.

I backed up and hid behind the bathroom door. I heard the lamp switch off, and a second later two sets of footsteps hurried up the stairs and past me, down the hall. There were a few more seconds of giggling before Gracie's door shut with a soft latching sound.

I leaned against the wall for a minute, then pressed my fingers to my lips, wondering what it was like to be kissed, wondering if I'd ever find out. I'd been jealous of my sister a thousand times over the years – she was the one with perfect vision, the more popular one, the more confident one. But it was more than that.

Gracie stayed out late. Gracie had boyfriends. Gracie went to parties and was going to college.

Gracie was getting out of Mursey.

And I was gonna be stuck here forever.

BO

We don't drive too far, just across the county line and a few miles down the highway. I mean to go farther, but the adrenaline's fading fast, and the late hour is catching up with me. There ain't no way I'm driving this tired. Not with Agnes in the car.

I pull into the parking lot of the first hotel I see. A giant, glowing sign tells us it's Sleepy's Spot. It's awful big, two stories, and seems as decent a place as any to catch a few hours of shut-eye.

'Where are we?' Agnes asks. She don't sound a bit tired.

'Hotel,' I say. 'Come on.'

'Shouldn't we keep going? We can't be far from home yet.'

'I'm too tired to keep driving,' I tell her. 'Your parents won't know you're gone until morning, and nobody's

16

.

gonna be hunting for me this late. If they are, they won't be looking outside Mursey yet. We got a few hours.'

Agnes clearly ain't so sure about this, but she don't argue. I get out of the car and unload Utah, who stretches and yawns before hopping out of the backseat.

'Grab our backpacks,' I tell Agnes. 'Don't bother with your cane. I'll guide you in.'

She tosses her white cane, folded up into a bundle of sticks, onto the floorboard. Me and Utah walk around the car and wait until Agnes's got one backpack slung over her shoulders and the other hanging from her right hand. I stare at the purple bag for a second, the one she brought with her.

'You didn't bring your phone, did you?'

'Of course not. Just clothes and money – like you said.'

'All right. Just making sure.'

She holds out her left arm, and I step forward, letting her grip just above my elbow, the way she'd taught me.

We don't say a word as we head across the parking lot, toward the automatic sliding doors of the hotel.

'Good evening,' says the man behind the desk, even though it's several hours past evening, if you ask me. 'How can I help y'all?'

'We need a room,' I say.

His eyes fall on Utah, and he stumbles backward, even though there's a tall counter between us. Like he's scared my dog, who's wagging her tail so hard she could clear a coffee table, might maul him. I oughta not be so hard on him, though. German shepherds do have real sharp teeth. And he don't know Utah would never use them.

He clears his throat. 'Ah. Well, do you have a reservation?'

'No.'

'I see . . . How old are you two?'

'Seventeen. Why?'

'I'm sorry, girls.' But he don't look too sorry to me. 'We can't let you rent a room from us.'

'Why the hell not?' I demand.

He narrows his eyes at me. 'Well, for one thing, we don't allow pets. But even if we did, all our guests are required to be at least twenty-one.'

'Are you fucking kidding me?'

'I'm afraid I'm not,' he says, and he sounds awful annoyed. Probably ain't used to being cussed at by teenagers in the middle of the night. 'And you'll find that's the case with most hotels in Kentucky. Now, if you have somewhere else to keep the dog and a parent or guardian who can—'

Me and Agnes are out the door before he can even finish that sentence.

'What do we do now?' Agnes asks when we're back in the car. 'We can't rent a hotel room – I think the twenty-one thing might actually be the law.'

'Then we'll find a place that'll break the law.' I know there must be places that'll rent to just about anybody. Too many girls get pregnant on prom night, and I know they ain't doing it at their parents' house. There's gotta be somewhere that'll let teenagers in.

We ain't driven five minutes when I see a place. Big red lights above the door read mot l – the e is burned out. The place looks run-down and dirty, even on the outside. The sorta place I'm sure a lot of drug deals have gone down in – many of them probably involving people in my family. If any place is gonna let two teenage girls rent a room, it's this one.

Beggars can't be choosers. Ain't that what they say? And me and Agnes aren't exactly on vacation. A shitty motel won't be the worst thing that's happened to us.

Well, not to me.

'Does this seem like a good place to try?' Agnes asks.

I'm glad she can't see the graffitied brick walls or the trash-covered parking lot.

'*Good* ain't the word,' I say. 'But this is where we're staying. Come on.'

Like I suspect, the man at the front desk don't give a damn about our age. Just as long as we pay in cash. Agnes takes some money out of her backpack, and we get a key to a room at the far end of the parking lot. He don't even ask about the dog. But when I unlock the door, I can see why. Utah can't make this place any worse than it already is.

The carpet ain't been vacuumed in years, and there are some mysterious stains on the wall I don't even wanna know about.

Agnes can't see none of it. She might be able to make everything out a little better if one of the lamps – the one on the desk – wasn't broken. I try to see the place through her eyes. Just a bed and a TV, with all the dirty details smoothed over.

'We should sleep,' she says. 'My parents will be up at seven thirty to get ready for church. I wanna be long gone before they come looking for me.'

'Or the police do.'

'They won't call the police. I left a note. They'll know it was me who took the car. They'll know it's not stolen. But they *will* come looking.'

I set the alarm for seven. Just three short hours away.

Somehow, the thought of waking up that soon makes me feel even more tired than I already am.

'I need to use the bathroom first.' She starts heading toward the bathroom, her arms outstretched, looking for the wall.

I don't help her. I know she can do it herself. But I do give her some advice. 'Hey, Agnes? Don't sit on the toilet, OK?'

'What?'

'Squat when you pee. Don't sit down.'

The look on her face makes me wonder if she's ever had to squat over a toilet in her life. Probably not.

But she don't argue.

While she's in the bathroom, I pull back the blanket. The sheets look all right, even though I'm sure nobody's washed them in days. Or weeks. I don't bother opening my backpack. I just slip off my cutoffs and climb into bed, wearing my T-shirt as pyjamas. Utah jumps on the bed and walks in a circle until she's made herself comfortable – right on top of my feet.

I grab the remote from the nightstand and switch on the TV. Most of the channels are just white fuzz, but eventually I find an infomercial on. Some old model advertising anti-aging face cream. That's as good as it gets this late at night. It's better than sleeping in the quiet.

Agnes comes out a second later. 'I squatted,' she says, like she's proud of herself.

'Good job.'

The queen-size bed is pushed up against the wall, so she's gotta climb over me to get to her side. 'You're gonna let the dog sleep in the bed?'

'Yeah. Why? She sleeps in my bed every night at home.'

'I don't know . . . Won't she get the blankets dirty?'

'No dirtier than they already are.'

I don't think she knows what to say to that.

'Bo,' she says after a minute. 'What are we doing?'

For a second, I'm scared, thinking she's changed her mind, thinking she might not wanna do this no more. Part of me wants that – wants to take her home, wants to keep her out of my mess – but another part of me, a bigger part, can't do this without her. I need her.

'I mean, what's our plan? Where are we going in the morning?'

I hold back a sigh of relief. Swallow it down a throat that's suddenly way too dry.

'Well . . . I thought . . . Maybe we could find my dad.'

'Your dad? How come?'

I sit up and switch off the lamp, so now neither of us can see. 'Money,' I say. 'He owes a shit ton of child support. Maybe I can get him to give me some money.'

'I guess that's not a bad idea. We'll need money if we're gonna make this work . . . This sure isn't how I imagined us getting out of Mursey.'

'Me neither.'

'We'll come up with a plan, though. Maybe . . . Maybe after we find your dad, we can try and get an apartment or something? Some place we can stay for a while. Until we turn eighteen, I guess. We'll have to figure out jobs and . . .' She yawns. 'I don't know. But once we're eighteen, we can go anywhere. We won't have anything to worry about. Right? Just you and me.'

Even in the pitch-black, I can't face her. 'Yeah . . . Right.'

'Do you know where your dad is?'

'No. But I'll find him,' I say. 'I got to.'

AGNES

I'll never forget the day Miss Bixley, the guidance counsellor, walked Bo Dickinson into my English class.

'Mrs Hartman,' she said, tapping on the open door. I knew it was her before she opened her mouth. Miss Bixley had the biggest hair I'd ever seen. It almost touched the top of the doorframe. Even I couldn't miss it. 'Sorry to interrupt, but I have a new student for you.'

'Oh?'

'Bo Dickinson,' Miss Bixley explained, ushering Bo into the room. 'I've decided to switch her into your class. I think this will be a better fit for her.'

By 'this' she meant the advanced class. Our school wasn't real big. Every high schooler in the county was bussed into Mursey, and we still had less than four hundred students. But we did have some honours and remedial classes. Maybe it was wrong of me, but I'd assumed Bo Dickinson would be in the latter. I'd just never thought of her as being advanced at anything school related.

And I clearly wasn't the only one. There was a sudden rush of whispers. They started quiet and got louder and louder, like a swarm of bees closing in.

'What?' Christy growled into my ear. 'There's got to be a mistake.'

Finally, Mrs Hartman cleared her throat and everybody went silent again.

'Glad to have you, Bo,' she said. 'There's an extra textbook on the shelf in the back. You can take whatever seat you find.'

'Thanks.'

As Bo headed to the back of the room, Miss Bixley called after her. 'Good luck, Bo. Thank you, Mrs Hartman.'

The classroom door shut, and Mrs Hartman cleared her throat again. She was a constant throat-clearer. She did it before almost every sentence. Sometimes loud, to get our attention. Sometimes not. But I always heard her.

'We're reading Robert Frost's "The Road Not Taken" today,' she explained to Bo. 'Page three thirteen. While Bo catches up with that, why don't the rest of you take another look, too, so you're ready to discuss in a few minutes.'

I didn't have a book – the print was too small for me to read, and using a magnifier was slow and a little exhausting. Instead, I just had a couple of pages Mrs Hartman had enlarged with the copy machine in the main office. A poem that took up less than a page in the book took up three sheets of paper for me. But at least I could follow along. Every once in a while Mrs Hartman would just read out loud whatever it was we'd be discussing, but I liked this better. I could underline or circle things I liked. Not that I ever understood any of it. I liked fiction, but poetry usually went right over my head.

Which is why I didn't raise my hand when Mrs Hartman cleared her throat and asked, 'So, what is this poem about?'

Christy raised her hand, though. She always raised her hand. Her arm brushed past mine as it shot into the air.

'Go ahead, Christy.'

'It's about being an individual.' Christy had on her sweetest voice. The one she reserved for teachers and Brother Thomas. 'It's about doing the thing no one else has done and how that can change your future.

"I took the one less travelled by, and that has made all the difference." It's a really lovely poem.'

'Nice job, Christy.'

'But that ain't what it's about.'

Everybody except me turned. This time, I recognized the voice. It was Bo.

'Yes, it is,' Christy snapped.

'Now, wait a second, Christy,' Mrs Hartman said. 'Let's hear Bo out. That's what this class is for, after all.'

I could tell by the crack in Christy's voice that she might be close to tears. She didn't handle correction real well. 'Sorry, Mrs Hartman.'

'Go on, Bo. What do you think it means?'

'It ain't about individuality or any of that. The road wasn't less travelled. He says it right there in the poem. "Though as for that the passing there had worn them really about the same." They'd both been travelled just as much.'

I looked down at my own copy of the poem. She was right. It said it right there, in the second stanza.

'Then how do you interpret the last line?' Mrs Hartman asked.

'You can't just look at the last line. It's that whole section there. He's talking about how he's gonna tell the story later – with a sigh and all that. When he tells it

27

years from now, he's gonna tell how the road he took was less travelled. It ain't about being different – it's about how we change our own histories.'

'OK . . . How do you mean?'

'Sometimes we tell ourselves stuff we know ain't true,' Bo said. 'Just to make us seem better or to give meaning to stupid things, I dunno. He says he took the road less travelled even though he knows he didn't. Just like some people tell everyone they're good little Christian girls, even though they're really gossiping, lying bitches.'

'Mrs Hartman, are you going to let her talk to me like that?' Christy demanded.

'She wasn't talking to you, Christy,' said Andrew, who was sitting on the other side of her.

'No. But I was talking about her,' Bo assured him.

The whole room began buzzing again, and I felt Christy start to stand up, but something yanked her back into her seat. Andrew, I figured. Although maybe I should've grabbed her, too.

'Enough,' Mrs Hartman hollered. 'Bo, that language will not be tolerated. Principal's office. Now.'

A chair scraped against the tile, and a second later Bo trudged past our desks, toward the door.

'Can you believe her?' Christy asked, her mouth close and hot next to my ear. 'Kicked out of class five minutes after she got here. Just what you'd expect from a Dickinson. And that was a stupid interpretation of the poem anyway.'

But the more I read the poem – and I read it several times that day and even again that afternoon when I got home – the more I thought she might be right. Maybe it was about the ways we rewrite our histories. And if that were true, how would I rewrite mine?

BO

I wake up with a cold, wet nose in my face and two big paws on either side of my head.

It's the same way I wake up every morning, and for a minute I forget where I'm at. I'm in my little twin bed back in Mursey. It's Sunday, and I ain't got nowhere to be.

'Not now, Utah.'

The words ain't even left my mouth when I remember. The voices on the police scanner, running through the woods, Agnes, the stolen car—

The goddamn alarm clock that was supposed to go off at seven.

I bolt upright and Utah scurries backward, then jumps off the bed, tail wagging and ears perked up.

'Agnes.' She's still fast asleep, her black hair fanned out over the pillow. She looks so peaceful that I almost

30

hate to wake her. But we gotta go. Now. I grab her shoulder and give it a shake. 'Agnes, get up.'

'Mmmm.'

'Come on. The alarm didn't go off. It's . . . shit, it's after ten. Get up.'

Her eyes blink open and she stares at me. 'You're still here,' she mumbles.

I act like I didn't hear her. 'Come on. Get up. We gotta go.'

'Ugh. OK, OK.'

I jump out of bed and pull on my shorts. Utah whines and nuzzles at my legs, wanting breakfast.

'Fine,' I mumble, grabbing my backpack off the floor and rushing to the bathroom. Hurry or not, I ain't gonna let my dog starve.

Last night, I'd packed some of her food into a ziplock bag, but I forgot to bring a bowl. I toss a couple handfuls of the kibble onto the bathroom floor. She starts chowing down before all the pieces even hit the ground.

'Good girl.'

I hear Agnes moving around in the other room, getting her clothes on. I get my toothbrush out of my bag and try to clean myself up as fast as I can. I look like shit. But I guess that don't matter right now.

'Bo,' Agnes says, and I can hear the shake in her voice. 'Bo, come back in here.'

'What?'

I step out of the bathroom and look at her. She's half-dressed, wearing just her jeans and a plain white bra. But she ain't moving. She's real still, her shirt loose in her hand.

'What?' I ask again.

She don't say nothing. Just points to the TV, still on from last night.

'. . . Atwood's parents contacted police this morning. It's believed the teenager may have run away with another girl, Bo Dickinson. Authorities say the vehicle is a silver Chevy with the licence plate . . .'

Mine and Agnes's most recent school pictures stare back at us from the screen while the news anchor talks, fast and monotone, like she don't give a damn what she's saying.

But I give a damn. I give many damns.

My heart starts beating so fast it hurts.

Agnes turns to look at me. Then she says what we're both thinking.

'Fuck.'

AGNES

I'd hoped to go to Lexington with my parents when they drove Gracie up to college. It'd mean two and a half hours in the car – one way – but I'd never been to a city that big. We could go to a real mall and eat at a nice restaurant. But my sister put an end to all those hopes when she packed two giant suitcases and a handful of boxes full of her stuff.

'How will you fit all of this in that tiny dorm room?' Mama asked as she lifted one of the cardboard boxes into the backseat, in the spot where I'd normally sit. There was just too much stuff and not enough room for four of us. Which meant I'd be the one left behind.

'I'll make it work.'

'Really? Because I'm not even sure we can fit everything in the car,' Daddy said, slamming the Toyota's trunk shut.

'Well, if you'd let me drive the Chevy and follow y'all up to campus . . .'

'Nice try,' Daddy said. 'You're not taking the car.'

'But it's *my* car,' Gracie whined.

'And yet, we're the ones paying for the gas. You don't need a car on campus. Not as a freshman. End of story.'

Gracie huffed and stomped her foot, but the way I saw it, she had nothing to complain about. She'd just gotten a huge scholarship to the University of Kentucky. She was getting the hell out of Mursey – something hardly anybody did. Around here, you grew up, got married, and stayed put. Going to college, especially a good state school like UK, was a big deal. Even in my family.

We weren't poor like a lot of people in Mursey. My great-granddaddy had opened a hardware store, Atwood & Son, way back when, and it had passed down to my daddy when Grandpa died, back when I was only three. Daddy owned the place now, and the business was doing well, so we weren't hard off. Mama stayed at home with Gracie and me, sometimes selling Mary Kay on the side. We never got to go on fancy vacations or anything, but we never wanted for anything, either.

We weren't well off enough that Daddy could pay for tuition at a state school, though. Lucky for my sister, she was one hell of a cheerleader – good enough to get the attention of UK, which had one of the best cheer programmes in the country. Her tuition was covered. Which made her the first Atwood to go to college.

And it made me the bitter, jealous sister.

Don't get me wrong, I was happy for Gracie, but she hardly acted like it was a big deal. Like everybody got to go to college for free. Like it was normal. But it wasn't. Not in Mursey. I was decent in school and didn't have an athletic bone in my body – and even if I did, our high school didn't have any sports that a blind girl could play. The chances of me getting a scholarship were pretty much zero.

The chances of me leaving Mursey were pretty much zero.

I didn't even get to ride along to drop her off.

'We'll be back tonight,' Mama said before kissing me on the cheek. We'd gone back in the house so she could grab her purse. 'Call your grandmother if you need anything. She can walk down here in about five minutes.'

'I know.'

'I'm sorry you can't come, sweetheart,' she said. 'I know you were looking forward to it. I had no idea your sister would be packing so much. There's just not enough room. Believe me. If I could replace one of those boxes with your butt in the backseat, I would. But Gracie—'

'Might kill you. I get it. It's OK. I'll see y'all tonight.'

'OK.' She kissed me on the cheek. 'Love you, Agnes.'

'Love you, too.'

Outside, Daddy honked the horn. Mama ran to the door and hurried out, hollering, 'Lock it behind me,' over her shoulder.

I couldn't help rolling my eyes. Lock the door? Mursey was hardly a dangerous town. My parents never even locked the garage door, so it wasn't something they were real worried about before. I doubted there were kidnappers waiting out in the bushes to take a blind teenager. But I didn't argue with her.

I never argued.

I tried to keep myself occupied once they'd gone. I turned on the TV, but there was nothing on besides sports, kids' cartoons, and some bad movies from ten years ago. I got one of the braille books Mama had ordered for me last year, and tried to read, but I was rusty. I'd gotten so used to reading enlarged text or using magnifiers that it took me twice as long to understand the raised dots on the pages. My mind kept wandering, and I had to rescan each line, my fingers sliding slowly along the page. Ten pages in, and I wasn't even sure what I'd been reading. I sighed and put the book back on the shelf.

Outside, I could hear a bobwhite whistling. I walked to the back door and pressed my face against the sun-warmed glass. Everything was washed in a blurry white haze. Like the brightness had been turned up way too high on the TV. I blinked a few times, trying to force my eyes to adjust. It was a pretty day, not cloudy at all, and with the summer fading fast, the temperature wasn't too awful. Warm, but not humid like the last three months or so had been.

It was a waste to stay inside on a day like this. I grabbed my cane and stepped onto the back porch. I stood on the top step for a long moment, shielding my eyes from the sunlight with my free hand. I wished I could've worn sunglasses, but I'd never found a pair that wasn't too dark for me to see through. Too much light was easier on my eyes than too little.

I wasn't even sure what to do now. Christy would tell me to lay out and get a tan while I still could, but my skin just burned and peeled anytime I was in the sun too long. Mursey was pretty rural, so there was nowhere to go besides the old woods behind the house. And Mama had always made me stay out of those woods. She said all the trails were grown over and it was too easy to get lost.

37

It was an old rule. One she'd made when Gracie and me were in elementary school and liked to play Pretend in the backyard. Gracie was always the princess, and I was always the servant girl. If Mama hadn't warned us, I'm sure my sister would've sent me out into the woods to fetch her something she needed to save the castle, better known as our garage.

But today, staring out at the trees, that old rule seemed awful silly. I was sixteen now, and I could walk in the woods if I wanted. Didn't matter that there was nothing back there but deer stands and old dirt-bike trails. If I couldn't go to Lexington, get out of Mursey, I could at least get out of the house. Mama couldn't be too mad about that.

And . . . I never had to tell her.

It was that thought that propelled me, cane in hand, down the back porch steps and out toward the woods. Under the cover of trees, my eyes adjusted a bit. My depth perception was still off and all the greens and browns bled together, but I was able to get my bearings and make out more than I had before. I managed to navigate through the thick brambles and high grass until I found one of the old paths that wasn't too overgrown yet. It was wide, like it had been used for four-wheelers before. I moved along slowly, swishing my cane back and forth, making sure not to trip over any tree roots.

Around me, I could hear all sorts of birdcalls. In the distance, a woodpecker was hammering away at a tree. Squirrels squeaked and bees buzzed around wildflowers so bright even I could see them. And not too far off, I heard twigs cracking beneath feet that were too small and fast to be human. The smell of grass and bark and dirt filled my nose and I inhaled it, glad for the fresh air. Nothing about the woods was unexpected – I knew what I'd find back here – I just didn't realize how peaceful or nice it would be.

I followed the trail for a while until it split into two narrower paths. I picked one at random and followed it until it split, too. I didn't think much about which way I was going. I was too taken with all the sounds and smells. I'd never really thought of myself as an outdoorsy person, but maybe I was wrong. Maybe there was something to all those poems Mrs Hartman made us read about the beauty of nature. I couldn't see much of it, but I could experience it. I ran my hands along tree trunks and smelled all kinds of flowers, wandering my way down the different trails until, all of a sudden, the sun hit my eyes again, and I found myself in the middle of a large, grassy clearing.

The grass was unkempt, nearly up to my knees.

I laughed and spun around in it for a minute, like a little girl in a movie, my hair swept up in the wind. It was silly, I guess. But I felt free. Like a dog who broke its chain. I was only in the woods behind my house. It was a small rebellion against a rule that hadn't been spoken in years. But it still felt good. Maybe better than it should've. So I spun and spun until I was so dizzy I could hardly stand up.

But then something dawned on me.

'Oh no,' I muttered, blinking at the woods around me. Several paths fed into this clearing, and after spinning around like an idiot, I'd lost which one I'd come in on. And even if I found it, I'd forgotten which paths I'd taken to get there.

And, of course, I'd forgotten my phone. It might not have helped much – Mursey had awful cell phone reception, and most people in town couldn't afford a cell phone anyway. My parents had bought me one for emergencies. Which seemed like a waste of money to me. I was always at home or with them. I'd never needed it.

But maybe I needed it now.

Because just like Mama had predicted all those years ago, I was lost.

My small rebellion didn't feel so good anymore.

I was still trying to decide which path to take back when I heard a shout and something coming up – fast – behind me. I turned just in time to see a huge grey blur speeding toward me. I didn't even have time to scream before it was on top of me, knocking me down and pinning me to the ground with its big paws. I yelped as a slobbery tongue began to lap at my cheeks.

'Utah!' a girl's voice hollered. 'Utah, get back here. Bad dog!'

The monster, which I now realized was a dog, backed off me with a whine and hurried back to its owner.

'You all right?' the girl asked.

I sat up, wiping doggy drool off my face. 'I think so.'

There was a pause before the girl said, 'Agnes?'

I blinked and tried to make my eyes adjust. I'd been too shaken to recognize the voice, but now, with my vision coming into focus, I saw the girl standing a few yards away. At least, I saw her red-gold hair.

Bo Dickinson.

I scrambled to my feet, embarrassed all of a sudden.

'What're you doing back here?' Bo asked.

'Just . . . taking a walk,' I said, trying to sound casual. That's when I realized I wasn't holding my cane anymore. I looked down, but the grass was too high for me to see anything on the ground. 'Crap.' I knelt

41

down and started feeling around for it.

'What's wrong?'

'My cane.'

'Oh.'

Then she was next to me, her hands bumping mine as they searched. With the added bonus of some sight, though, she had better luck finding it.

'Here.' She put the cane in my hands, and we both stood up. 'Sorry about Utah. She just likes people a whole lot.'

As if to illustrate this, Utah began rubbing against my legs, her tail wagging hard enough that I thought she might bruise my calves.

'It's OK,' I said, stepping back from the dog. 'She just startled me. I'm not real used to dogs. We've never had one, and big ones make me nervous.' I didn't know why I was telling her all that. Bo Dickinson probably didn't give a damn about my anxiety around dogs.

'All right,' Bo said. 'Well, Utah and me oughta be heading back, so . . .'

'OK,' I said. 'See you at school, I guess.' I looked back at the woods and swallowed. Now I was really embarrassed. 'Actually, Bo?'

'Yeah?'

'Can you . . . Can you help me?' I tried to smile.

'I took the path less travelled and didn't fare quite as well as Robert Frost.' Bo was quiet for a long moment, and I realized she might not know what I was saying. 'I'm lost,' I admitted. 'I can't remember how I got here, and—'

'Oh. OK. You want me to walk you back to your house?'

'You . . . know where my house is?'

'I've spent a lot of time out here,' she said. 'I know where all the paths go. Come on.'

I followed her out of the clearing and back into the trees, Utah the dog running along beside us. Part of me was paranoid she'd turn and jump on me again, and I wished Bo had her on a leash. I stared straight ahead, watching Bo's wild hair as it wove between trees, guiding me like some sort of fairy in a children's story.

Neither of us spoke for a while, then, out of nowhere, Bo broke the silence. 'Can I ask you something?' I didn't have time to answer before she went on and asked anyway. 'What's wrong with your eyes?'

'Um . . . well, I'm legally blind.'

'I know that. I ain't stupid. I mean, why? Were you in some kind of accident as a kid or . . .?'

'No. I was born this way,' I said. 'It's called Leber's congenital amaurosis, but doctors usually call it LCA.

43

It's genetic. My parents carry the gene and just didn't know it until they had me.'

'So they can't fix it?'

'Nope. Not as far as we know.'

This was the part where people usually said something like 'I'm so sorry' or 'Wow, Agnes, you're such a trouper.' But Bo didn't say a word. She just kept walking, not bothering to warn me about tree roots or uneven ground. She didn't need to, that's what my cane was for, but most people still did.

We didn't say anything else until we reached the end of a path, and Bo stopped, letting me catch up to her. 'That's it,' she said. 'Straight ahead is your backyard.'

'Thanks,' I said. 'It would've taken me forever to get back.'

'No problem. Come on, Utah.' She turned and started walking away, down the wide path, but I called after her.

'Bo?'

'Yeah?'

'How come you were in the woods behind my house?'

'Because,' she said. And I thought she might laugh. 'They're the woods behind my house, too.'

BO

'You said they wouldn't call the cops!'

'I didn't think they would – Bo, slow down.'

'We gotta get the hell out of here.'

'Yeah, but getting pulled over won't do us any good.'

She's right. I take a deep breath and ease up on the gas. Utah whimpers in the backseat. She's probably curled up in a ball, scared half to death by my frantic driving. I'm a real piece of shit.

I make a sharp turn, and the Chevy swerves onto a bumpy back road. We gotta get off the highway.

'I should've known,' Agnes says, her voice about to break. 'I told them not to call the police in my note, but I should've known they wouldn't—'

'It don't matter,' I say. 'All that matters is that we get as far away from Mursey as we can. Before someone sees us. Goddamn it. We were on the news. We're so fucked.'

'Maybe . . . Maybe not a lot of people watch the Sunday news? I mean, a lot of people are still in church.'

'Yeah, in Mursey. But that's a tristate news channel. There were more than enough people watching to catch us.'

The car bounces and jitters along the gravelly road. My teeth clack against each other. My mind is spinning. We gotta do something. More than just get out of Mursey – we gotta make sure we ain't recognized.

'We gotta ditch the car.'

'What?' Agnes squeaks.

'They said the licence plate number on the news,' I tell her. 'We gotta ditch the car.'

'How will we get anywhere?'

'We'll get a new car.'

'Where?' she asks. 'How?'

I don't answer. I ain't sure yet.

Then I see a house up ahead. A little grey house with a metal fence and a yellow Lab in the yard. Out front, an old man is sitting on his porch, drinking something out of a mason jar. Tea, maybe. Or beer, even though it's early. A clock never stopped none of my family from drinking.

But it's the car in his driveway that catches my eye. An old piece of junk, really. It's grey and boxy and the doors are dented all to hell.

46

I slow the Chevy down.

'What are you doing?' Agnes asks.

I roll down the window. 'Excuse me, sir?'

The man don't notice us at first. He just keeps drinking and tapping his foot on the concrete steps of his porch. Maybe he's blind, like Agnes. Or deaf. Or maybe he's just ignoring me.

I shove my palm into the steering wheel and the horn blares. Next to me, Agnes jumps and covers her ears with her hands.

The man looks up this time.

'Sir,' I holler out the window. 'Sorry to bother you.'

Oh Lord, I hope he ain't seen us on TV.

'Yes? Can I help you with something, darlin'?'

'You sure can.' I try to sound sweet, the way Agnes does, but it don't taste right in my mouth. It sounds like I'm being sarcastic or mean or mocking.

The old man gets to his feet. He adjusts his ball cap before walking – real slow – down the steps and toward the road.

'Bo,' Agnes says in my ear. 'What are you doing?'

'What is it you need, sweetheart?' The old man leans forward, resting his weight against the fence. Behind him, the yellow dog is running from one side of the yard to the other. Back and forth. Over and over.

47

I keep my sweet smile on and gesture toward the old piece of shit in his driveway.

'I'd like to buy that car from you,' I say. 'Right now. If it runs.'

'Bo,' Agnes says through gritted teeth. 'What the hell?'

I ignore her and keep my eyes on the old man. 'What do you say? Let me take the piece of junk off your hands.'

'Sorry, sweetheart. That car ain't for sale,' he says.

'Come on. I'd be doing you a favour.'

'That's one of the first Plymouth Reliant Ks ever made. It's an antique.'

'It's a garbage can on wheels,' I argue.

'I told you. It ain't for sale.'

'Not even for . . .' I do some quick math in my head. 'Not even for eight hundred dollars?'

Next to me, Agnes gasps. I swallow hard, but I don't look at her.

The old man changes his tune real quick. 'Eight hundred?' he asks. He knows as well as I do the car ain't worth half that. 'Hmm. Well, I don't know if I can part with it for less than—'

'I'm not gonna haggle with you, sir.' I ain't even trying to be sweet no more. It wasn't doing me no good anyhow. 'Eight hundred and no questions. Take it or leave it.'

'All right. Sold.'

'Thought so.'

'Bo,' Agnes says again, this time louder. 'What are you doing? What are you thinking?'

'I'm getting us a new car.'

'But—'

'Trust me.'

Lucky for me, she does.

Not that she should.

I park the Chevy in the old man's driveway, next to the battered car. He tells us his name is Earl before heading inside to get the keys. Me and Agnes grab our stuff from the backseat while Utah and the yellow dog paw at each other through the fence.

'Are we just leaving my sister's car here?' she asks.

'It won't take them long to find it,' I say.

The front door opens, and Earl comes back out of his house, keys jangling at his side.

'Wait here,' I tell Agnes. She nods and leans against the shitty car, arms folded over her chest.

'Y'all must be in a hurry,' Earl says while I unzip my backpack and hunt for the cash I've hidden inside. 'You gotta be teenagers. Why do you need another car so bad?'

'I said no questions.' I pull out the wad of cash I'd tucked into an inside pocket. Carefully, I count out eight hundred dollars. That's most of it. Way more than I wanted to spend this early. 'Here,' I say, shoving the money into Earl's hands and taking the keys from him.

'Pleasure doing business,' he says, fingering the wrinkled bills.

'There's another thing.'

Earl raises an eyebrow. 'I ain't got nothing else to sell you, girl.'

'That car – the one we're leaving – it's stolen. If you wanna call the police and let them know it's here, that's fine. But, please, don't tell them nothing about us.'

'Police? What are y'all getting me into?' Earl demands. 'I ain't gonna lie for two strange kids.'

'I'll give you another fifty bucks.'

'Seventy-five.'

'Fine.'

'I never saw you. Far as I know, that car was just dropped off here when I woke up this morning.'

I hand him a few more bills, then tuck the rest of the cash back into the backpack.

'Y'all take care now,' Earl hollers as I walk back toward Agnes.

I unlock the Reliant K and load Utah into the back while Agnes climbs into the front seat.

'Just gotta do one more thing,' I tell Agnes. She shrugs.

I walk back to the Chevy and slide into the front seat.

The keys are still in the ignition. I leave them there and, instead, pop open the console. There are a bunch of fast-food napkins inside, but I manage to find a red ink pen, too.

On a Wendy's napkin, I scribble a note to Agnes's parents. They'll find it when they come get the car.

Mr and Mrs Atwood – I know you hate me, but I had to. I'm sorry. Bo

AGNES

'Still feels strange not having Gracie at the table,' Mama said, scooping mashed potatoes onto my dinner plate. 'I'm so used to cooking for four, we always have so many leftovers now.'

'Nothing to complain about,' Daddy said around a mouthful of pork chop.

Gracie had been gone for about two weeks, and the house did seem awful quiet lately. Mama called her every night and made her talk to Daddy and me, but Gracie always tried to rush off the phone pretty fast. She had to study or hang out with her new friends or go to cheerleading practice. She had a million things to do and a million places to go.

Me? I hadn't left the house since the day I'd wandered around the woods, except to go to school. Christy was always busy with Andrew, and no one else ever invited me anywhere.

'How's school going, Agnes?' Mama asked, finally sitting down next to Daddy.

I shrugged.

'Use your words,' Daddy teased.

'It's fine. English is the only subject I'm any good at, and all we've been doing is reading poetry, which usually doesn't make much sense to me. So that's been hard.'

'What about math?'

'It's geometry,' I said. 'Blind girls and shapes? Not the best combination.'

It was meant as a joke, but my parents took it very seriously.

'Are your teachers making accommodations for you?' Daddy asked.

'Should we call the guidance counsellor? Or the principal?' Mama asked. 'If you need more help—'

'No, no. I'm OK,' I said. 'I was mostly kidding. The shapes are hard, but my teacher's great. I've gotten OK at doing proofs.'

'If you do have any issues, though, you'll tell us,' Mama said. 'We can always have them take another look at your IEP.'

An IEP was an individual education plan. My parents and teachers and members of the school board met every year to make adjustments to it. That's where they figured out what equipment and accommodations I needed, and what the school could afford to get me.

'Can you pass the green beans?' I asked Daddy, hoping to get off the subject.

Whenever my school and accommodations came up, my parents usually got angry. They always insisted the school should do more for me. 'If they can spend all that money on the football team, they can get you the materials you need,' Mama would say. Maybe she was right, but the truth was, I was doing fine with what I had. New tape recorders and giant glass magnifiers would just make me feel even more awkward at school.

Luckily, Daddy had other things to talk about. 'My mother stopped by,' he told Mama. 'She wanted me to remind you that you agreed to take her to her doctor's appointment tomorrow afternoon.'

'Oh shoot,' she said. 'I forgot. That means I won't be able to pick up Agnes from school.'

'I can't, either,' Daddy said. 'Rodney's got the day off, and I can't leave the store.'

'What do we do?'

'I can take the bus,' I offered.

'Mmm . . . I don't want you walking all that way,' Mama said.

'It's not that far.' The school bus didn't come down most of the side roads of Mursey. Instead, it dropped a bunch of kids off at the church, which was just around the block – or straight back through the woods, but I wasn't trying that again. All right, so it was a big block and part of the way didn't have any sidewalks, but it still wasn't too bad. 'We walk there every Sunday. I know the way.'

'I don't know,' Mama said.

'Can't Christy drive you?' Daddy asked. 'She's got a car now, right? I thought I saw her nearly run over Mr Jordan in the gas station parking lot a few days ago.'

'She's not that bad of a driver,' I said. And then, on second thought, added, 'Well, she's getting better.'

Daddy laughed.

'That's a good idea, though,' Mama said. 'Christy can drive you home, then y'all can hang out here for a while. She can even stay for dinner if she wants.'

'And as long as she doesn't run anybody over,' Daddy said, 'we don't have to worry about how you'll be getting home.'

'I don't see what there is to worry about,' I said. 'It ain't that far.'

'Grammar,' Mama warned.

'It's not that far,' I amended. 'I've had mobility

training. I know how to cross a damn street.'

'And language,' she scolded.

'Someone with your mouth doesn't deserve to walk home alone,' Daddy joked.

'And now that that's settled,' Mama said, even though I wasn't sure it was, 'who wants dessert?'

When she left the table to get the pie Grandma had dropped off, I looked at Daddy. For a second, I thought of asking him why me taking the bus was such a problem. I didn't mind riding home with Christy, but walking home didn't seem like it ought to be a big deal.

But I couldn't say anything. Gracie was the arguer. Not me.

So Mama came back and put pie on our plates, and we talked about the hardware store and the grocery list and the high school football team . . .

And the subject was completely forgotten.

At least until the next day, when I had to ask Christy for a ride.

'Sorry, Agnes. I can't,' she said.

'Why not?'

'I'm going over to Andrew's house.' Christy picked a soggy french fry off my tray, thinking I wouldn't see. I always did, but for some reason, I never called her out on it. 'His parents are coming home late, and –' she leaned across the table so that I could hear her whisper – 'I think today's the day. I think we're going to . . . you know.'

'To . . . what?'

'You know . . . sleep together.' She sank back into her chair.

'Oh . . . wow.' I shoved a fry in my mouth and took a while to chew, just to give myself a minute to think. Finally, I swallowed. 'I thought y'all were waiting for marriage?'

'Don't be all judgy,' she said, annoyed.

'I'm not. I'm just surprised. You were so set on it before.'

'It's not like I'm turning into Bo Dickinson or anything. It's just . . . I mean, Andrew and me, we're practically married as it is. He's getting me a ring for Christmas. He already told me. He'd do it sooner, but our parents . . . Anyway, we'll probably get married summer after graduation. Might as well get some practice in first.'

I nodded, even though, deep down, the idea of Christy marrying Andrew, the only guy she'd ever dated, right after high school made me sort of uneasy for the both of them. And I wasn't really sure why.

It wasn't like it was unusual. Most people in Mursey were married before they turned twenty-one. It was just the way of things. It'd probably be my way, too, if any guy ever actually wanted to marry me. If I didn't get married shortly out of high school, I'd be stuck in my parents' house forever.

Those were your only choices around here. Go to college, which hardly anybody had the money to do, or get married. And Grandma had already told me I ought to be looking now. 'You're gonna need someone to take care of you,' she'd told me more than once. The idea of me taking care of myself had never come up.

But the thought of dating just one boy, of being with just one person from the time you were a teenager until you died . . .

Maybe Bo Dickinson had the right idea, sleeping around the way she did.

'Why can't you take the bus?' Christy asked.

'My parents don't want me walking home from the church alone.'

'Are you kidding?' she asked. 'Don't you make that walk every Sunday? It's not that far.'

'Yeah, but they're worried.'

Christy was quiet for a second before she said, 'I like your parents, Agnes. But they really are overprotective sometimes. You've got to stand up to them more.'

'I know,' I said. 'But they're not that bad. And I can't

really blame them. I'd probably be worried, too, if I had a blind kid.'

'I don't know,' Christy said. 'I think they're being ridiculous. And I think you ought to just take the bus home anyway.'

'That's what I want to do. But Mama would be furious.'

'Who says she has to know?' she asked. 'You'll be home before she is.'

Which was a good point. And it wasn't like I had any other options. Most of our friends didn't have cars – they rode the bus, too.

'Look,' Christy said, 'if she asks, tell her I drove you. I'll cover for you if I need to.'

So that afternoon, I made my way out to the parking lot and climbed on the school bus for the first time in my life. That little spark of rebellion was flaring up again, and I felt almost giddy. Riding a bus wasn't exactly breaking the law, but it was definitely a bigger deal than my wandering in the woods that day. At least in my parents' eyes. That had been an old rule, one that had faded and blurred over the years. This one was new and sharp and clear. And I was going against it anyway.

Trouble was, I hadn't really thought about what I would do once I was on that bus.

Everything inside the bus blurred together. Kids in

blacks and browns blended into their seats, making it hard for me to tell which seats were taken and which were up for grabs. It wasn't the first time I'd wished camo wasn't such a popular fashion choice in Mursey. I blinked, hoping the sunlight coming through the windows would help once my eyes adjusted, but that was taking too long for the driver.

'Sit down,' he said. 'We gotta go.'

'OK. Sorry.' I started to move toward a seat near the front that, as far as I could tell, was empty.

'In the back,' he snapped. 'Front seats are for the middle schoolers. High school students sit in the back.'

I gulped and started walking, my cane snagging on the edges of people's shoes and backpacks. I hoped the back seats would look clearer once I got closer, but they were still blurry. The only difference was, I could hear people whispering – probably about me – in some of them.

The bus driver honked the horn and hollered back at me, 'Sit down.'

Maybe this was a mistake. Maybe I should've just called Daddy and made him leave the store for a minute. Or Mama could've gotten one of her friends from church to come. Or I could've begged Christy to put off losing her virginity just half an hour longer so she could drive me home.

'Agnes.'

I almost didn't hear her over my own panic. Her voice wasn't loud at all. But when I looked to my right, the sun was pushing through the dirty glass just enough to glint off a mane of strawberry-blond hair.

'Sit down,' Bo said.

'I can't see where—'

'Sit here,' she said.

'Oh.' It wouldn't have been enough to say I was surprised. Sure, she'd helped me out in the woods, but the bus was school grounds, and Bo Dickinson and I weren't friends. If anything, I'd have thought she hated me the way she hated Christy.

But the bus driver slammed his hand on the horn again, and I was left without a choice, so I sat.

'What're you doing on here?' Bo asked. 'Don't your mama usually pick you up?'

'How did you know that?'

'I've seen y'all in the parking lot a thousand times. Not all of us are blind, you know.' She nudged my arm in a way that was almost playful. After a second, though, she said, 'Sorry. Was that a bad thing to say? I ain't always sure what's . . . what do you call it? Politically correct?'

'You're fine,' I said. 'Honestly? Sometimes I forget other people can see stuff like that.'

61

'Makes sense. You've never known no different, so . . .'

The bus started moving, and for a few minutes, neither of us said anything. I thought the whole bus ride might be that way, and I wasn't sure if I was relieved about that or not. But before I could figure it out, Bo started talking again.

'You didn't answer,' she said. 'What're you doing on here?'

'Oh. Um . . . my parents were both busy this afternoon. So I'm taking this to the Baptist church and walking home.' For a second, I considered telling her I'd been told not to, like Bo might be impressed by my rule-breaking streak. First the woods, now this.

But Bo was the kind of girl who cussed in front of teachers and stole her mama's whiskey to bring to parties and went down on other girls' boyfriends. None of my little rebellions would be at all impressive to her. If anything, she'd probably just laugh at me.

I wasn't sure why I cared about impressing Bo Dickinson, but the idea of her thinking I was some kind of loser really bothered me.

'Hey,' she said. 'You read that poem for English yet?'

'The Dylan Thomas one? Yeah. I don't get it, though. I mean, it sounds pretty. "Rage, rage against the dying of the light." It's nice, but it doesn't make sense to me. What is the good night?'

'Death,' Bo said. She didn't say it the way Christy would, like I was some kind of idiot. She just put it there, an answer.

'Death,' I repeated.

'He's telling somebody to keep fighting and not just die,' she explained. 'I read somewhere that he wrote it about his dad.'

'Wow. You're really good at poetry stuff.'

'Nah. I just . . . I like it. Poetry, I mean. I wish I could write it, but I'm no good.'

'Write it?' I laughed. 'I'd be glad if I could just understand it. I like fiction. I like a story. But I have to read every poem a thousand times, and I still never really get it.'

'It's not a real useful skill,' she said. 'Not like math. Now, that goes over my head. Junior year, and I'm taking algebra for the third time. Who cares if you know what the hell Robert Frost is talking about after high school? Math actually matters.'

'I could help you with algebra.' The words came tumbling out before I could stop them. It was just instinct. Habit. I'd been good at algebra freshman year and I'd helped half my class pass Algebra II last year.

I'd offered to help a lot of friends with their math. But Bo Dickinson wasn't my friend.

I didn't hang out with girls like Bo.

And she didn't hang out with girls like me.

'Maybe,' she said. 'And I could help you with poetry.'

'Maybe.'

Another long pause while the bus bounced along. The roads in Mursey hadn't been fixed in a long while. Some hadn't even been paved yet. On the streets that weren't dirt or gravel, you still had to deal with huge potholes and uneven concrete.

'Hey, Bo!' a boy yelled from a few seats back. 'What're you doing this weekend?'

Bo didn't answer.

'Wanna hang out?' the boy asked. 'I'll give you ten bucks and some whiskey if you'll come over and suck my dick.'

Bo spun around in the seat, almost knocking me into the aisle. 'Fuck off, Isaac.'

Isaac Porter. The quarterback. I was surprised to hear him talking that way. He sat in the pew behind us every Sunday with his grandparents. He'd always seemed real polite.

'What's the problem?' he asked. 'You do it for every other guy in town. Why not me? Is my dick too big for your mouth?'

I could hear some of his buddies laughing. I cringed. I wasn't naive or anything. I'd watched plenty of R-rated movies with Christy and we'd talked about sex and stuff before. But I'd never had a boy talk to me the way Isaac was talking to Bo. Hell, I'd never heard a boy talk to any girl quite like that before.

'Keep telling yourself that, asshole,' Bo said. 'Fucking redneck.'

'All right, well, I'll just ask your mom, then,' he replied. 'She'll do it for five.'

I thought Bo was gonna climb over the back of the seat then; her sharp elbow jabbed my shoulder as she lunged. But the bus came to a screeching halt, throwing everybody forward and sending Bo slamming backward into the seat in front of us.

'You OK?' I asked.

'Fine.' She took a minute to right herself while people walked past us, toward the door. 'Come on,' she said. 'We're here.'

'You get off at the church, too?'

'Yep.'

I slid out of the seat and Bo followed.

'Bye, Bo,' Isaac called. 'See you at my place tonight.'

'I hate the people around here,' Bo said as we stepped

off the bus, onto the sidewalk in front of the church. 'People like him and Christy – fake motherfuckers – I hate them so goddamn much.' She paused and took a breath. 'Sorry.' I thought she meant about bringing Christy into it, but then she added, 'I probably shouldn't say *goddamn* in front of the church, huh?'

'Probably not.'

The bus pulled away, and everybody started walking home. But Bo and I just stood there, staring up at the cross above the door. It was big and white, and even I could see it pretty clearly.

'Can I ask you something?' But, again, she didn't wait for my answer. 'Do you believe in all that stuff? God and Jesus and all that?'

'Yeah,' I said, taken aback. 'I mean . . . I think so. I guess I've never really thought about whether I believe it or not. What . . . what about you? Do you believe in it?'

'I want to,' she said. 'But then I think . . . if there is a God, he's done forgot about the Dickinsons.'

I didn't know what to say to that.

After a second, Bo turned and started walking, and I did, too, my cane clicking on the sidewalk behind her. It was a sunny day, but a little cloudy, which meant it was just the right amount of brightness for me to see at my best. I could make out more details than usual – like the empty kiddy pool in one of the yards we passed and Bo's short, scrawny frame, slouched as she walked along in front of me.

'You live over here?' I asked.

'Yeah. The trailer down there on the corner.'

'Oh.' Suddenly it all made sense: her walking past the church that day, her in the woods. She lived in the trailer my grandmother always pointed out on the way to Sunday school. I knew Dickinsons lived there, but I hadn't realized Bo was one of them. 'We're practically neighbours.'

'Sorta,' she said. 'If you go straight into the woods from my back door and head a little to the left, you can be right behind your house in ten minutes.'

'It scares me that you know that.'

She laughed and slowed down so that I could walk next to her. 'Told you – I spend a lot of time out there. I also know how to take the trails to Sally Albert's house in fifteen minutes. I've been skinny-dipping in her pool at midnight before. She'd shit herself if she knew.'

'Skinny-dipping with who?'

'Everybody, if you believe what people say.'

'Should I?' I asked. 'Believe what people say?'

She took in a breath, like she was about to answer, but then, out of nowhere, she just stopped. I'd taken a few steps before I realized she wasn't walking with me. I looked back.

'Bo?'

'Shit.' Then she moved past me, faster than before, toward her front yard. It was still a couple houses down, so I wasn't sure why she'd taken off like that. Not until I heard her holler, 'Mama!'

I hurried after her, thinking something was wrong. I almost tripped a few times – it was hard to use the cane properly when you were moving too fast – but I managed to reach Bo's house just a second after she did.

'Mama,' Bo said, moving onto the grass. 'What're you doing?'

I squinted, scanning the space in front of me, trying to get a better focus. Bo's trailer with its rickety wooden front porch. An old car in the gravel driveway. A lawn mower sitting next to a huge oak tree. And that's when I saw her – Bo's mother. She was so skinny it was no wonder I'd missed her, even on a bright day like this. She had dark brown hair pulled back into a low, scraggly ponytail, and she was wearing a black tank top that made her skin look almost paper white. Maybe they looked more like each other in the face – I couldn't make out details like that – but from what I could see, she hardly looked like Bo, with her strawberry-blond hair and tanned skin.

That's when I remembered that Bo's mother had married into the Dickinson family, and I had no clue who she'd been before that.

'Bo,' Mrs Dickinson said. 'Good. You can help me. I'm gonna fix the lawn mower.'

'When was the last time you slept, Mama?'

'I'm fine. I just gotta fix the lawn mower.' She waved her hands in the air, and I noticed she was holding something silver. I glanced down and saw several more little silver objects at her feet, reflecting the sunlight. Tools, I guessed.

'It ain't broke, Mama.'

'I can make it run better,' she said. Her voice was shaky and quick, like she was anxious and excited all at once. And she couldn't seem to sit still. It made it hard for me to keep focus on her. 'I can take it apart and put it back together and—'

'You ain't even used that thing in years,' Bo said. 'The county has to come and do it half the time. Mama, let's just go insi—'

'Shh!' Mrs Dickinson snapped. 'Wait.'

'Wait for what?'

'They're watching,' Mrs Dickinson whispered. She took a couple steps toward the oak tree and looked up. 'They're up there. They're watching us. Can't you see them?'

'No one's watching, Mama. Let's go inside.'

Mrs Dickinson let out a yell and flailed her arms. I only knew she'd thrown one of the tools when I heard it clatter onto the sidewalk a few feet away from me.

'Damn it, Mama!' Bo shouted. 'Stop it! You could've fucking hit somebody!'

'I was aiming for the people in the tree,' Mrs Dickinson said. 'Who's that on the sidewalk? Who's that girl? Is she watching us, too? Is she with them?'

I stood there, confused and wondering if I should go. But now Mrs Dickinson was coming toward me and I didn't know whether to run or introduce myself. I opted for the polite thing.

'Hi,' I said. 'I'm Agnes. I go to school with—'

Bo stepped in front of me, blocking her mama's path. 'She ain't with nobody. There's nobody in the trees. You're acting like an idiot.'

'Shut your mouth!' Mrs Dickinson yelled. 'Don't you dare talk to me that way. You're my daughter. I'm the adult. Stop acting like a little bitch, you hear me?'

I flinched. How could a mother call her own daughter a bitch? Then again, Mrs Dickinson didn't seem like your average mother, and Bo didn't even seem fazed. When she spoke next, her voice was calm. Calmer than I'd ever heard it.

70

'Come on, Mama,' Bo said. 'Let's go inside. If they're watching, we can close the windows. They can't see inside.'

'But I wanna fix the lawn mower.'

'We'll do it later,' Bo said. 'Come on. Before the neighbours call the cops.'

I stood there, frozen, as Bo ushered her mother to the trailer. I knew I was watching something that ought to be private. Something I ought not be a part of. But I was rooted to the spot. Maybe it was concern for Bo. Maybe it was just my own nosiness. Either way, I didn't have a clue what to make of everything I'd just seen and heard.

Bo didn't look back or say anything to me as she urged Mrs Dickinson, who was still twitching, onto the rickety wooden porch. I waited, hoping she'd turn around and say something before they went inside. Tell me that it was gonna be OK or just say goodbye or . . . anything, really.

But all I got was the slamming of the screen door behind them.

BO

'I know I'm white trash and all, but this is extreme, even for me.'

I pick up the rusty scissors we found in the Reliant K's glove compartment and laugh, but Agnes just gives this half smile. She ain't said much since we bought the shitty car a little over an hour ago, and it's making me nervous. What if she's changed her mind? What if she wants to go back home? Can't say I'd blame her. Especially considering where we're at right now.

The truck stop bathroom smells like sweat and piss. Soggy paper towels litter the sticky floor, and the walls are smeared with graffiti. Agnes don't gotta see to know this place is a dump. But it's the best we got for now.

'You sure about this, Bo?' she asks.

'Our pictures were on the news. We gotta make ourselves look different somehow.'

She nods and turns to face the mirror.

'Don't be nervous,' I say. 'Mama used to cut hair out of our trailer when I was little, and she taught me some. I had to cut her bangs.'

She makes a face, and it's clear this ain't much comfort.

I step behind her, scissors clutched in my hand. Her coal-black hair is so long, almost to her waist. I take a deep breath. 'Here we go.' I start at the back, cutting slowly and carefully. She's taller than me, so I gotta stand on my tiptoes. Locks of hair fall around us, getting on my T-shirt and in my mouth.

I remember doing this for Mama years back, before Daddy left. Remember her laughing as Daddy opened a beer and said, 'That little girl's gonna put your damn eye out if you ain't careful.'

'I trust her more with these scissors than you,' Mama said. 'Don't care if she's eight or eighty-seven.'

When I was done, Daddy took a look at my work. 'Well, shit, Bo,' he said. 'Ain't too bad.'

'Can I cut your hair next, Daddy?' I'd asked.

'Maybe after a few more beers,' he said, chuckling as he kissed me on the top of my head.

There were a few nights like that when I was little. Where we'd all be laughing and talking and being nice to

73

each other. Maybe even eating dinner together. Like I imagined the other families in town did. They'd only last for so long, though. Then, usually, both my folks would end up getting drunk and yelling at each other. But they started out good, at least.

Most of those good nights ended when Daddy left.

I spit some of Agnes's hair onto the floor and keep cutting until I've given her a shoulder-length bob. It ain't as pretty as before, but it ain't terrible. 'Turn around.'

She does.

'Close your eyes.'

She does.

I use my fingers to comb her hair in front of her face. I take a few careful snips. The scissors are dull, so they don't cut quite right. But I manage to give her bangs. Long ones that stop just above her eyes. They ain't even, but they're good enough. She don't look like the same clean-cut girl no more. Not at first glance anyway.

'Done.'

She steps away from me and looks in the mirror. I don't know how much she can see, but the look on her face tells me she ain't thrilled. She runs her fingers through the strands around her face and sighs. I wait for her to say something. Maybe make a joke. But she stays quiet.

I swallow. 'All right. My turn.'

'What?'

'You gotta cut my hair now.'

'Bo, I can't,' she says.

'Yeah, you can.'

'I'm blind.' She says it like I've done forgot.

'It ain't gotta be pretty.' I put the scissors in her hand.

'What if I cut off your ear?'

'You won't.'

'But your hair,' she mumbles. 'It's how I recognize you.'

'I should've cut it off forever ago. It's always in the damn way. And you'll find another way to recognize me. Just do it, all right? I wanna get out of this shithole.'

'Fine.'

I use both hands to smooth my hair back into a ponytail and hold it in one fist. 'Cut the whole thing off.'

'OK.' She steps closer. Her left hand slides along my face and neck. Eventually, her fingers settle over mine, gripping the ponytail while she chops at it. My hair is thick and wavy, and it takes a while to chop off the whole thing. When she's done, I feel almost dizzy with the loss of all that weight.

I take the scissors from her and look in the mirror while I even up the sides a bit. When I'm done, it's all I can do not to cry. Despite everything I said before,

I hate this. My hair was a pain, a mess, but it was the only thing about me that was pretty. Now it's choppy, cut to my ears, and I look like a little boy. Short and skinny and awkward.

I ain't gonna let Agnes know how upset I am, though. She'd feel guilty, even though I'd asked her to do it.

'Not bad,' I lie. 'If we get caught, at least we'll have some killer mug shots.'

She smiles, but just barely.

I ain't used to this. To her being so distant. It's got me scared, but I don't got the nerve to ask her about it. Instead, I clear my throat and say, 'All right. Let's get the hell out of here.'

We walk out of the bathroom, leaving piles of golden, red, and black hair on the floor.

AGNES

I spent the next two weeks waiting for Bo.

Waiting for her to walk into English class. Waiting for her to come down the sidewalk, past the church, on Sunday morning. Waiting for her to say something – anything – to me.

I was always watching for her, keeping an eye out for that golden mane of hair to come around the corner. I saw her almost every day, but we didn't say a word to each other for two weeks.

Then, on a Friday afternoon, I'd decided to spend my lunch period in the library. Christy was out sick, so I didn't have anyone to sit with. Besides, I had a research paper due in World History that I needed to work on. I'd taken a seat at a table near the checkout desk so that Mrs Dalker, the librarian, could help me find books if I needed her to. For now, I'd picked a

77

book about the black plague.

If I wanted to read any normal-size books without having a bunch of pages copied and enlarged in the front office, I had to use this giant crystal-like magnifier. It was shaped like a dome and at least two inches thick. I had to slide it along the page, leaning close to read each word I passed over. It was slow going, but I'd gotten used to it.

What I hadn't gotten used to was the way other people acted about it.

'What the hell is that thing?'

Before I could do anything to stop it, a hand swooped down and swiped my magnifier right out from under my nose. Literally. I looked up, but I didn't recognize the boy in front of me. He had dark hair and wore camo, but that could've described about half the boys in my high school.

'Can I have that back, please?'

'What the fuck is it?'

'A magnifier,' I said. 'I need it to read.'

Without warning, he grabbed my book, slid it across the table, and bent over. 'Well, goddamn. You're blinder than I thought, Agnes. Ain't gonna lie. Always kinda thought you were faking it, but fuck – this thing is strong.'

'Uh . . . yeah.' It wasn't the first time someone admitted they'd thought I was faking. But I still hadn't figured out how to respond to it.

'Give it back to her, Garrett.'

I whipped around, but I didn't have to look to know. I'd been waiting – hoping – to hear that voice.

Bo Dickinson was behind me.

'Come check this out,' Garrett said. I knew who he was now. Garrett Bishop. A sophomore. He was in the Future Farmers of America with Christy and Andrew. Until now, he'd never said more than two words to me.

'Stop being a fucking dumbass and give back the magnifier,' Bo said.

'Or what? You'll go tattle on me? Thought you were cooler than that, Bo.'

'I ain't gonna tattle,' Bo said. 'But I will tell your girlfriend that you tried to feel me up at Andrew's party.'

'She ain't gonna believe you.'

'You sure about that?'

But I guess he wasn't, because, after about a second, he shoved the book and the magnifier back over to me and started to walk away. I thought I heard him mumble, 'Fucking bitch,' as he headed for the library door.

Bo, who never seemed fazed by the names people threw at her, plopped down in the chair across from mine.

'Thanks,' I said.

'No problem. He's an idiot anyway.'

'Did he really try to feel you up?'

'Yeah. Spilled beer down the front of my white shirt, too. Still ain't convinced that was an accident. Kinda a waste, though. Not like I got the boobs to rock a wet T-shirt.'

'But I thought you were . . . At Andrew's party, I heard you . . .'

'Went down on Perry Schaffer in the hayloft?' Bo asked. 'Nah. Perry just told a bunch of people that. And then your best friend went and told everybody. Speaking of, shouldn't you be eating lunch with her right about now?'

'She's sick. I think she's got strep throat.'

'Too bad,' she said. 'Listen. You know how you said you could help me with algebra?'

I nodded. 'Yeah.'

'Well . . . I understand if you ain't got time . . . or if you just don't want to, but I was wondering—'

'I'd be glad to,' I said, then felt mortified by how fast the words had tumbled out of my mouth. I shouldn't have sounded so excited to help her with math. She'd think I was some kind of freak.

But, if anything, Bo just sounded relieved. 'Thanks.

I just . . . I got a test coming up, and I really don't wanna take this class again. So maybe I can come over this afternoon?'

'Uh . . . to my house?'

'Yeah. That all right?'

'Sure. Of course.'

'Great. I'll walk over from the bus stop later, then.'

The bell rang, and Bo and I hopped to our feet. I put my library book and my magnifier in my backpack before we headed toward the doors.

'By the way, how's your mom?' I asked. 'Is she OK?'

'What do you mean?'

'Well, the other day she just seemed . . . I thought maybe she was sick or needed some kind of medication or . . .' All of a sudden, I felt awkward. I shouldn't have brought it up. It was none of my business.

But then Bo was laughing. At least, I thought she was. The sound was darker. Bitter.

'Medication's the last thing she needs.'

'What do you mean?'

'She's fine. She was just tweaking.'

'Tweaking?'

'Yeah. You know, zooming . . . on meth.'

'Oh.' I stopped and readjusted my backpack on my shoulder, trying to process what she'd just said. Meth.

Crystal meth. I'd never seen anybody on drugs before. I'd never even seen anyone smoke pot. At least, not that I knew of. A lot could happen without me noticing. But still. I'd never really even thought about meth. The idea of someone's mom doing it blew my mind.

'Don't know why you're surprised,' Bo said. 'Ain't uncommon around here.'

'It's not?'

Bo snorted. 'You really are blind,' she teased, slapping me on the arm. Then she headed off down the hallway, calling over her shoulder, 'I'll see you after school.'

BO

'Where'd the money come from, Bo?'

My hands tighten around the steering wheel. 'What money?'

'The money you bought the car with,' Agnes says. 'Where'd it come from?'

I take a deep breath. In the backseat, Utah shifts and lets out a long, bored groan. We're all stuck in this car, and there ain't no way I can avoid this question. I'm surprised it took this long for her to ask in the first place.

'I . . . I stole it.'

'What?'

'Mama's been dealing,' I say. 'Has been for the last few months. I knew where she was keeping the cash, so I took some before I left.'

'Oh,' she says.

She sounds awful relieved. Like she expected me to

say I'd robbed a liquor store. Guess I can't blame her. That's the kinda thing people in my family do. I used to think I was different, but in the last twenty-four hours I'd taken my mama's drug money and stolen a car. A Dickinson through and through.

'But if you have money, why do we have to find your dad?' Agnes asks. 'Aren't we looking for him so we can get some money?'

I keep my eyes on the highway, letting the pavement and the road signs fill my vision. I can't look at her. I can't lie to her face.

'It ain't enough,' I tell her. 'We just spent most of it on the car. What I got left ain't enough to live on long. We still gotta find my dad if we wanna stay gone till we're eighteen. We're gonna need money for all kinds of shit. Like . . . gas and rent if we wanna find a place to stay . . . Mama didn't have that much saved.'

I'm sure it sounds flimsy coming out of my mouth, but it's good enough for Agnes.

'Right,' she says. 'That makes sense.'

My hands relax, and my foot eases up on the gas. I hate that I'm relieved. Part of me wishes she'd called me on my bullshit. That she'd demanded I take her back home.

I just can't stop thinking of her parents and how

much they gotta hate me now. There are about a million other things that oughta be on my mind, but that's what I keep coming back to. I can hear the names they're probably calling me. Can hear their voices cursing my name up to the high heavens.

Maybe if they'd never let me into their house, this wouldn't be happening. Maybe if I'd never gone over there to work on my algebra, Agnes would still be at home, instead of in a shitty car with a bad haircut and fifty dollars of stolen drug money.

I hadn't even cared about the algebra anyway. I'd just . . . wanted to hang out with her.

I wish I could regret all of it, but the truth is, if none of that had happened – if I didn't have Agnes now – I ain't sure I'd have had the nerve to run. Despite everything I'd always said, all the promises I'd made myself, I probably would've just sat there in the trailer, waiting for the cops to come. Because I couldn't do this alone.

I couldn't do this without her.

Even if I feel awful about dragging her into my mess.

'OK,' she says. 'So we don't know where your dad is, right? How do we find him?'

I shake my head and clear my throat. 'I know someone who can tell us where Daddy is. We're about there now.'

I turn off at the next exit. A couple stoplights and five

minutes later, we're pulling into the parking lot of an apartment complex. It ain't fancy, but it ain't a hellhole, either. Half the lawn out front is brown and dead. A few of the cars are old and dinted, but others seem all right. And the parking lot ain't too dirty. Just a few crushed beer cans on the concrete by the Dumpster.

It's no paradise, but it seems safer than the motel we stayed at last night. That's for sure.

'Get your stuff,' I say as I climb out of the Reliant K.

'We're staying?'

'Hope so.' I put Utah's leash on and grab my bag. Agnes's cane clicks on the concrete behind me as I lead the way to one of the ground-level apartments. I knock on the door, the branches of a cheap wreath scratching my knuckles. 1B is the only door with any kind of decoration on the outside.

'Who lives here?' Agnes asks.

Before I can answer, the door swings open and a tall, skinny boy is standing there. He's got a mop of reddish-blond hair and eyes like sweet tea. Eyes that can only belong to a Dickinson. And right now, they're staring, real wide, right back at Agnes and me.

'Bo? What are you—?'

'Hey, Colt,' I say, giving him a half-guilty smile. 'I need a favour.'

AGNES

'So x would equal fifteen.'

Bo stared down at the paper where I'd been working the problem with a thick black marker. 'Wow,' she said. 'Seems a hell of a lot easier when you do it. Mr Ryan makes it look so hard.'

'Yeah.' I capped the marker and dropped it onto the dinner table. 'He's not real clear when he teaches. And he'd always forget to make large copies of the homework when I had his class, too. Mama ended up going down to the school to give him a talking-to more than once.'

'Seems like your mama really fights for you.'

'She does. It's embarrassing sometimes.'

'I think it's great,' Bo said. 'If I was you, I wouldn't be embarrassed at all.'

And, like she'd been summoned, Mama and her big blond hair appeared in the kitchen doorway. 'Sorry to bother y'all *again*.' She probably didn't emphasize the *again*, but I sure heard it that way. This was the fourth time she'd come out of the kitchen in the past hour, always with some excuse for why she needed to poke around the dining room for a few minutes.

When I'd told her Bo Dickinson was coming over, she'd been surprised, to say the least. But she hadn't said no. Or tried to discourage me from spending time with Bo. Which, honestly, I'd half expected her to do. My parents had never been as outright hateful toward the Dickinsons as Grandma was, but still. Bo Dickinson wasn't exactly the girl parents around here wanted their kids hanging out with after school.

I think she was winning Mama over, though. She'd been real polite since she got here, and even complimented the cookies Mama had made from scratch. And now, my guess was, Mama had just overheard our conversation about Mr Ryan and how Bo didn't think she'd done anything embarrassing by confronting him. I imagine she probably liked that an awful lot.

'You girls need anything?' Mama asked. 'Some tea or more cookies, maybe?'

'No, thank you, Mrs Atwood,' Bo said.

I shook my head. Just like I'd done when she'd asked fifteen minutes ago.

'All right. Well, if you change your mind, just let me know. I'll be in here on the phone with your sister, Agnes. I'll tell Gracie you said hello.'

'Thanks, Mama.'

When she left the dining room again, Bo said, 'That reminds me. I gotta call my cousin and make sure he's still taking me to Dana's party tonight. You coming?'

'Coming . . . where?'

'To Dana's party.'

'Oh.' I shook my head. 'No. I don't really go to parties. They're usually pretty dark, and my vision is even worse when there's not much light. It's just too much of a pain for Christy or someone else to guide me around all night, so . . .'

'I'll do it,' Bo said.

'Do what?'

'Jesus, you don't listen for shit, do you?' She laughed. 'I'll guide you around all night. I don't mind.'

'Oh. No, that's all right. I couldn't be a burden.'

'You ain't a burden,' Bo said. 'Come on. It'll be fun.'

It was something I never in a million years thought would happen – Bo Dickinson sitting in my dining room, inviting me to a party. And it certainly wasn't something I'd ever thought I'd want to say yes to so badly.

It wasn't a good idea, hanging out with Bo. People

89

would talk. I was having a hard time caring about that as much as I ought to, though. Because I'd never been to a party before, and the idea of going with someone like Bo, someone who didn't treat me like deadweight or a thing to be pitied . . .

'Mama?' I hollered. 'You on the phone yet?'

She was back in the doorway in half a second. 'No, but if I was, yelling at me would be awful rude, now wouldn't it?'

'Sorry,' I said. 'Can I go to a party at Dana Hickman's tonight? With Bo?'

'Oh. Um . . .' She hesitated, and I wished I could see the details of her face, be able to use that to know what she was thinking. 'Well . . .'

I felt a little guilty all of a sudden. I could tell by Mama's voice that she didn't want to say yes. Of course she didn't. I was asking to go to a party with a Dickinson. But I'd put her on the spot by asking in front of Bo. There was no easy way to say no.

'Uh . . . Will there be parents there?' she asked.

'I think so,' Bo said. Though, from everything Christy had told me about the parties she'd gone to, that seemed real unlikely.

'Well . . . uh . . . I guess that'll be OK.' She sounded a little defeated. 'But you'll have to be home by ten thirty.'

I frowned. When Gracie was my age, she'd been allowed to stay out until eleven – sometimes twelve – on the weekends.

'Can I use your phone?' Bo asked. 'I gotta call my cousin and make sure he's still driving us.'

'Oh. Sure. It's in the kitchen.'

'Thank you, ma'am.' Bo stood up and headed through the door.

After a second, Mama asked in a quiet voice, 'Will Christy be at this party?'

'Um, I doubt it,' I said. 'She was out sick today. Strep throat.'

'That's too bad,' Mama said. 'I was just . . . Bo knows you can't see real well when it's dark, right? Will she be able to help you get around? She knows not to just walk away or—'

'She knows,' I said quickly.

'All right. Well, if something happens, you call me, OK? I'll be right there.'

I nodded. 'OK, Mama.'

I sure didn't remember Gracie getting this many questions before she went to parties.

A second later, Bo came back. 'He's gonna pick us up here at seven,' Bo said. 'If that's all right with you, Mrs Atwood?'

'I suppose that'll be all right,' Mama said.

It wasn't even five o'clock yet, which meant we had two hours to hang out and get ready.

Well, I got ready. Bo said she was just gonna wear the shorts and tank top she'd had on at school that day. But me, I had to try on about six different outfits. I sure wasn't going to my first party in beat-up jeans and one of Mama's hand-me-down shirts. Maybe it was silly, since I'd just seen all these people at school, but I wanted to look nicer. Prettier.

Maybe . . . sexier?

I shook that thought away. It didn't matter what I wore. I was still the slightly too tall, slightly too chubby girl with the white cane. No one was gonna think I was sexy. And, even if they did, I wasn't sure there was anybody in Mursey I wanted to find me sexy.

After a lot of going back and forth, I decided to embrace the last breath of summer and picked out a yellow sundress Mama had bought me last year. It fell just above my knees and had halter straps that tied behind my neck. I loved the way it hugged my curves, and even though Gracie used to tell me I was too pale to pull off yellow, it was my favourite colour.

I pulled my hair into a long ponytail and put on my nicest black sandals. Then I turned to face Bo, who'd been sitting on my bed, flipping through my braille books and asking me questions about them for the past two hours.

'What do you think?' I asked.

Bo hesitated. 'Well . . . It's nice. But you look like you're going to homecoming, not a party in someone's backyard.'

I groaned. 'I'll change.'

'No, no,' Bo said, hopping to her feet. 'You look real nice. You should wear what you want. Besides, I think my cousin's downstairs. I see his truck through your window.'

I grabbed my cane and followed her downstairs. Daddy was home now, sitting in the recliner, watching TV. 'Hey, honey,' he said. 'I hear y'all are going to a party. Sounds fun.'

'Yep.' I gave him a quick kiss on the cheek. 'See you tonight, Daddy.'

Bo and I were almost out the door when I heard Mama's voice from the kitchen.

'Whoa, whoa, whoa,' she hollered before coming into the living room. 'Just a second, girls. Bo, you said your cousin is gonna be driving?'

'Yes, ma'am.'

'And I can trust him to be safe, right?'

'Yes, ma'am.'

'And he'll have Agnes home by ten thirty.'

'Uh-huh.'

'Maybe I should come out there – meet him myself. Let me get my shoes.'

'Oh, let them go, Maryann,' Daddy said. 'I'm sure Bo's cousin will get them there fine. If you want Agnes home by ten thirty, she'd better get going.'

I'd never felt so grateful to Daddy in my life. But then he said: 'The Hickmans don't live far from here. If we get worried, we can just drive over there and check on her.'

He laughed.

I didn't.

'OK,' Mama said, clearly resigned. 'Just be careful. No drinking, no drugs—'

'I know,' I said. 'Bye, y'all.'

'Goodbye, Mr and Mrs Atwood,' Bo said as we headed out the front door and onto the porch.

It was already too dark for me to see much. The crickets and a few cicadas, still clinging to the dying summer, were singing their night songs. Two headlights shined from the driveway, giving me just enough light to follow Bo, who led me to the passenger's side of a tall pickup truck.

She opened the door and climbed in. I folded up my

cane and hoisted myself in beside her, trying to keep my skirt down. The truck was tight quarters, but Bo was tiny enough to fit between me and the driver.

'Agnes, this is my cousin,' Bo said, 'Colt Dickinson. He just graduated in May.'

Even though Bo had said her cousin was driving, it hadn't occurred to me until just now that I'd be going to the party with two Dickinsons. Which probably should've worried me far more than it did.

'Hey, Agnes,' said a boy's voice from behind the wheel. I couldn't see him at all, but I could already imagine the head full of strawberry-blond hair he must have, just like the rest of his family. 'I was in the same class as your sister. Gracie at college now?'

'Yeah,' I said. 'UK.'

'Good for her.'

'Come on,' Bo said. 'Agnes's gotta be back by ten thirty. Y'all can get to know each other at the party.'

None of us said much on the ride to Dana's house. Colt had the radio tuned to a country station, and I caught myself humming along to a Tammy Wynette song as the truck bounced down gravel roads. Dana Hickman lived all the way across town, but Mursey was so small, it only took about five minutes to get there.

We parked half a mile or so from the party. Bo said

too many cars in front of Dana's house would draw a lot of attention and the cops might come. I hadn't even thought about that, the idea that the cops might come. The thought made me nervous.

And maybe a little bit excited.

'Let's go,' Bo said, urging me out the door. I slid from the truck, unfolded my cane, and started following her down the dirt road.

'Hey,' Colt called after us. I heard the truck door slam and keys jangle. 'I can't even get a thank-you?'

'Thanks,' Bo hollered over her shoulder, but neither of us stopped walking.

There was the sound of quick feet behind me, and then Colt was at my side, laughing in a way that was almost musical. 'What're you gonna do when I'm gone and can't drive you to parties no more?'

'I'll find someone better to drive me.'

'Where are you going?' I asked him.

'Nowhere special.'

'He's being modest,' Bo said. 'Colt's leaving town in a couple months. He's got a welding job lined up in Louisville.'

'It ain't in Louisville,' Colt said. 'It's about forty-five minutes from the city. It's nothing special, like I said.'

'Sounds special to me,' I told him. 'You're getting out of Mursey. That's pretty special.'

'You think so?' Colt asked.

'Definitely.'

'Which means it'll be up to me to carry on the Dickinson legacy in this town,' Bo said. 'Now I gotta get in enough trouble for the both of us.'

'I don't think that'll be too hard,' Colt said. 'Whatever you don't do, the town will say you did anyhow.'

'Ain't that the truth.'

I shifted, readjusting my grip on the cane. I wasn't sure how to respond to any of that. I'd grown up believing all the stories I'd heard about the Dickinsons. Believing they were trash. And I knew at least some of the stories were true. Meeting Bo's mama had proved that. But the way Bo and Colt talked, not every story should be believed. I wondered how much had been made up and how much was real. And had I been part of spreading any of the lies myself? The thought turned my stomach.

We were getting close to the party now, though, and we all stopped talking as the sound of voices and country music grew louder. Bo looped her right arm through my left and led me around the side of the small house; Colt was a few paces behind us. I couldn't see much as we rounded the corner, into the yard, but the smell of smoke filled my senses, and a few minutes later, I saw the bright glow of the bonfire.

'I'm gonna grab a beer,' Colt said. 'Agnes, you want one?'

'Uh . . . no,' I said, shaking my head. 'Thank you, though.'

'You sure?' Colt asked.

I wasn't. But I was too embarrassed to say so.

I nodded.

'All right,' he said. I thought he'd ask Bo if she wanted one next, but he didn't. Instead, he just added, 'I'll catch up with y'all in a bit.'

'Take your time.' Bo took hold of my arm again and pulled me away, toward the bonfire. 'Here's a chair,' she said, guiding me into a half-broken lawn chair. 'Can you see at all?'

'A little bit,' I said, folding my cane up and putting it in my lap. 'The light from the fire helps some.'

Bo flopped down on the grass at my feet. 'Can you see me?'

'Sort of. Mostly just your outline. It's too dark for me to see your face. Oh, and I can see your hair.'

Bo laughed. 'Even a blind girl can see Dickinson hair.'

I smiled. 'It's true. That's how I recognize you most of the time. Your hair and your voice.'

'You know my voice?' She sounded excited by this.

My face felt warm all of a sudden, and I didn't think it

had much to do with the fire. 'Yeah,' I said. 'I mean, it's how I recognize most people. I have to spend a little time with them before I can really remember it, but—'

'Agnes?'

It took me a second to put a name to that voice. I'd heard it before, I knew it, but I wasn't sure it had ever spoken directly to me. It was a voice I'd heard in passing – in the hallways, giving an answer in class – a thousand times, though. And I figured out who it was about half a second before Dana Hickman was standing in front of me, blocking out the light from the fire.

'Holy shit. It is you!' Dana was talking way louder than necessary, and she smelled like beer. A lot of beer. 'The hell're you doing here?'

'Am I not supposed to be here?' I asked.

'Nah. I didn't say that! Just surprised is all. Christy said she never brings you to parties because you're always clinging to her – you know, 'cause you can't see? It's gotta be so annoying for her. Nice that she helps you out most of the time, though. Where is she, anyway?'

'Um . . .' I swallowed, not wanting Dana to see the tears I felt coming on.

No. Fuck it if Dana saw. Bo. I didn't want Bo Dickinson to see me cry. Not over something stupid like Christy calling me clingy. I wanted her to think I was tough.

A badass, like her, not a weak, weepy crybaby.

'She didn't come with Christy,' Bo said from the grass. 'She came with me.'

'Oh shit. Bo, I didn't even see you down there,' Dana shouted. 'Now, I knew *you'd* be here.' She laughed, her whole body swaying, and I felt a splash of something cool on my feet. Beer, I realized. 'You're always at the party, ain't you? Always fucking somebody. Who's it gonna be tonight?' She didn't say it mean, the way Christy would have, but like she was actually curious. Still, her words made me cringe.

'Ain't decided yet,' Bo said, voice cold and flat.

'Hey, Dana,' Colt said, next to me all of a sudden. 'Somebody's looking for you over by the cooler.'

'All right. I need another beer anyway.'

'No, you don't,' Colt muttered as Dana stumbled away.

'You know Dana?' I asked him.

'Yeah. Her brother's my age. He ain't got much filter when he's drunk, either.'

He sat down on the grass and started talking to Bo. Well, I guess he was talking to both of us, but I wasn't really listening. I was still thinking about what Dana had said. Of course Christy had called me clingy. She'd said it herself, that guiding me around a party when she had other things to do was a burden. I couldn't really blame her. Who wanted to lead a blind girl around all night? I felt a rush of guilt, of shame, because Bo might have insisted I wouldn't be a burden, but now that we were here, I was sure she felt different. Sure she wanted to be free of me.

'Hey,' I said, cutting Bo off midsentence. 'If . . . if y'all wanna go do something, I can just sit here.'

'What're you talking about?' she asked.

'You know. It's a party. I'm sure just sitting here isn't much fun. Y'all can go dance or talk to other people or—'

'If just sitting here ain't much fun, why the fuck would we leave you here?' Bo asked.

'I just—'

'And if you're bored sitting, we can fix that,' she said.

'I'm not— That's not what I was—'

'This is one of your favourite songs, ain't it, Colt?'

'Sure is,' he said. 'Gotta love Hank Jr.'

'Well, then. Maybe y'all should dance.'

'Oh, I can't—'

'I think that's a great idea,' Colt said. He took a long swig of beer, then tossed the cup aside before standing up. 'Come on, Agnes.'

'No, really. I'm fine. You don't have to dance with me, Colt. Besides, you can't really dance with a cane.'

'I know I don't got to,' he said. 'But we're gonna dance anyway.'

'And you don't need the cane,' Bo said, swiping it from my lap. 'I'll hold on to it.'

'But—'

'Don't worry,' Colt said. His hand was on mine, pulling me to my feet. 'I got you.' I was about to open my mouth again, but he squeezed my hand and repeated, this time almost a whisper, 'I got you.'

He was careful as he led me away from the fire. The farther we walked, the less I could see, until the shadows all melted together and darkness swallowed everything whole. But Colt's hand stayed around mine, warm and reassuring.

I was being led into darkness by a Dickinson boy. A voice in the back of my head – which sounded an awful lot like my grandma's – told me this could not end well. But I didn't feel nervous. Not the way I should've. And when Colt stopped and pulled me toward him, his other hand resting on my waist as he eased me into the beat of the music, I let myself relax, trusting that, even though I couldn't see a thing, he had me.

'This isn't so bad,' I said.

'Well, thank you.'

I laughed. 'I didn't mean it that way. Just that . . .

102

I haven't really danced with anyone before. Except my daddy at his cousin's wedding, but I was about six and he let me stand on his feet. And it wasn't this dark.'

'I'm glad to be your first real dance, then,' he said. 'So, you ready?'

'For what?'

'This.'

He dropped his hand from my hip and spun me around. I squealed as my hair whipped around me and my feet stumbled. But just when I thought I'd trip, his hand was on me again, catching me, pulling me back toward him.

And I was laughing.

'Warn me next time,' I said.

'I thought I did.'

'I hope no one's staring.'

'And I hope they are,' he said. 'Here's your warning.'

He spun me again, but that time I kept my footing. So he threw me another curveball, swinging me out, away from him, then pulling me in again. I was laughing so hard that I did trip that time, and he caught me by the elbow.

'Sorry,' he said. 'Should I stop?'

'No,' I choked. 'You shouldn't.'

We danced like that through a few more songs, Colt

singing along to the lyrics about honky-tonks and whiskey while he swung me around. I laughed until I could hardly breathe, but I kept my feet moving, barely able to keep them on the ground. I loved the way my dress twirled around my thighs, the feel of the cool, late-summer air on my skin. It felt like I was flying.

'Incoming!' Colt called.

I didn't have time to ask what he was saying before he flung me away from him again, but this time he let go. I sailed away from him, my body still spinning, until I crashed into something slim and solid. I toppled to the ground, my legs and arms tangling with the person I'd spun into.

I wasn't sure how I knew – the smell of her skin or maybe just her size – but I was sure even before we fell into the grass that it was Bo I'd collided with.

'Shit,' Colt said, standing over us. 'I'm so sorry. I thought you were gonna catch her and—'

But Bo and I were both laughing too hard to hear him.

She was stuck half-beneath me, and I rolled off her so we were both sprawled in the grass, laughing so hard it hurt.

'Are y'all OK?' Colt asked.

'Think so,' Bo said, panting. 'Jesus, Colt. I was coming over here to tell y'all you looked crazy. You didn't have to throw Agnes at me, though.'

'If you were gonna be an asshole, I did. What about you, Agnes? You all right?'

'Never been better,' I said.

And I kind of meant it.

'Shit!' someone yelled from across the yard. 'Cops!'

'Fuck,' Colt said. 'We gotta go.'

'Yep.' Bo hopped up, then she pulled me to my feet. 'Run.'

'What?'

She answered by taking off at top speed, her hand still gripping mine. My feet scrambled at first, startled by the sudden movement, but I caught my balance.

It's hard to make yourself run when you can't see. Your brain tells you to stop, that it's not safe. I hadn't run in years. I'd barely walked outside my house without a cane. And a cane wasn't much use if you were sprinting.

My legs were longer than Bo's, and it wouldn't be too hard to keep up if I could just push past my instincts, if I could just let myself run with her. I kept my legs moving, kept my fingers locked with Bo's as we ran into the cornfield. I stumbled over the terrain, shocked by the brush of stalks against my bare legs. I focused on the rhythm of my feet slapping against the ground, trying to keep it and my breathing steady instead of thinking about the fact that I was literally running blind.

And, eventually, I fell into it. The panic faded away, replaced by exhilaration. I hadn't moved this fast in maybe my whole life. The air was rushing past me; my dress and my hair were blowing behind me. For once, I wasn't focusing on navigating my way through the dark, on what was ahead of me.

I thought dancing with Colt had felt like flying, but I was wrong. This was flying.

'Not much farther to the truck!' Colt hollered from behind us.

'We're almost there,' Bo told me.

But I didn't care. I didn't care how far the truck was. Or that I was running from the police – with two Dickinsons, no less.

None of that mattered because, for that moment, running through the cornfield, holding tight to Bo's hand – I felt alive, I felt wild, I felt . . .

Free.

BO

'What the fuck were you thinking, Bo?' Colt yells so loud it makes Agnes jump beside me. He's pacing the tiny living room of his apartment, and I worry for a second the neighbours might hear the shouting.

'Cut the shit, Colt,' I say, keeping my voice low. 'You'd have done the same thing, and you know it.'

'I sure as hell wouldn't have dragged Agnes into this, though,' he snaps.

'Excuse me,' Agnes says, sitting up straighter on the couch. It's the first time she's spoke since we got here. 'It was my choice to come with her. Bo didn't make me do anything.'

Colt sighs and runs his hand through his mop of hair while Utah rubs against his legs, desperate for attention now that he's stopped yelling. 'All right. So . . . what? Y'all steal a car, cut off your hair—'

'It wasn't really stealing,' Agnes argues. 'It was my sister's car.'

'And we bought the car we got now.'

Colt ignores us. 'So now what? What's your plan? Where're y'all going? Don't tell me you're thinking of staying here. I love you, Bo. More than anything. But I just got my shit together, and if the cops come looking for you here and I get in trouble—'

'Relax,' I say. 'We ain't asking to stay. Except maybe for tonight. We ain't even asking for money.'

Colt sinks down into the battered old armchair across the room. Utah hops right into his lap, like she's some sorta prissy toy poodle, not a full-grown German shepherd. He strokes her ears while he talks. 'Then why're you here?'

'I'm looking for Dad.'

'Your dad?'

I nod.

'Bo, I ain't got a clue where he's at.'

'But Uncle Jeff might.'

Colt groans. 'Bo . . .'

'Come on. Please?'

'I ain't talked to him in over a year.'

'But you got his number, right?'

'Wait,' Agnes says, looking between us. The living

108

room is bright enough that I figure she can probably see OK. 'Who's Uncle Jeff?'

'My dad,' Colt says.

'Oh.' She looks horrified. 'You still have his number? I thought he was awful to you and your mama before he took off.'

'Yeah. He was.'

'But he's the only one my dad would keep in touch with,' I tell her. 'They were real close growing up. After Daddy left, he'd still call Uncle Jeff. Tell him to say hi to me. Sometimes he'd even send him money to give me for Christmas. Just, like, twenty dollars or something. He'd never send it to Mama because she'd just spend it on . . . Anyway, I know Uncle Jeff'll be able to get ahold of him.'

'So you need me to call my dad.' Colt sits back in the chair, and Utah whines when he stops petting her. 'Why're you looking for Uncle Wayne anyway? What's he got to do with y'all running away?'

I stare down at my lap. At my dirty, bare knees. Because I can't look at his face. Or Agnes's. 'He's got money,' I say. 'And that's what we need right now.'

'And you think he'll give it to you?'

I nod.

'This is a dumb plan, Bo.'

I grit my teeth and look up. 'Colt—'

'The whole thing is stupid. Running away, looking for Uncle Wayne – it ain't gonna end well.'

'And you think me turning around and going home will end much better?' I ask. 'You know what would've happened if I stayed. I ain't going through that again, Colt.'

'Bo—'

'And it's only gonna be worse now that I done took off,' I tell him. 'You might think it's a dumb plan, but I can't go back.'

Colt nudges Utah off his lap and stands up, walking toward the kitchen. 'Agnes?' he asks. 'You wanna beer?'

'Uh . . .' She glances at me, then back toward the kitchen. 'Sure. Thank you.'

'Does that mean you'll call Uncle Jeff?' I ask.

'I guess.'

'And we can stay here tonight?'

He walks back into the living room, two cans of beer in his hands. He gives one to Agnes, then pops the top on his own. 'Fine,' he says to me. 'Y'all can stay tonight. But that's it. I'll get in a lot of trouble if the cops come looking for you here.'

'They won't,' I say.

And I sure hope I'm right.

They think I'm asleep.

I'm curled up on Colt's ugly couch, a blanket pulled over me. The TV is on, turned down low, while *The Tonight Show* plays. But Agnes isn't on her camp-bed on the floor. She got up a while ago and went to Colt's bedroom.

They think I'm asleep, but I can't sleep. And these walls are real thin.

'I'm sorry,' Agnes says. 'About your dad. I didn't know that was Bo's plan.'

'My dad's not what I'm worried about,' he says. 'Agnes, I know y'all are close, but—'

'But nothing. I couldn't let her go alone. I know you think I'm stupid.'

'I don't think you're stupid at all,' Colt says. 'I'm glad you love Bo. For a long time, I've been the only one looking out for her.'

He's selling himself short. Colt didn't just look out for me growing up, he practically raised me. Especially after Daddy left. Colt was the one I ran to when the rumours about me got too mean. Colt was the one who remembered to tell me happy birthday when Mama didn't. Colt was the one who brought bread and cheese to the trailer so I'd have something to eat.

For a long time it was just me and Colt against the

world. Or at least against the town of Mursey.

'I can't take care of her anymore,' he says. 'Now that I'm here . . . she needs you.'

'And I need her.'

'But, Agnes . . . what about school? What about graduation? You're smart. You could—'

'I'm probably not going to college anyway,' Agnes says. 'I'd graduate and then, what? Be stuck in Mursey? Live with my parents until I marry some redneck I went to school with? What's the point? What's the point if Bo's not there?'

'But what're you gonna do?' he asks. 'Y'all gotta make money somehow, right? How're you gonna do that?'

'I . . . I don't know. Maybe I could teach braille somewhere? I don't know. I'll figure it out. Bo and I will figure it out.'

'I just . . . I don't want you getting hurt.'

'Bo would never hurt me.'

'She'd never mean to,' he says.

My fingers knot in the thin blanket as a weight sinks down onto my chest. Utah grumbles in her sleep and shifts her position on my feet.

'I like you, Agnes,' Colt continues. 'I don't wanna see you dragged down by the Dickinsons. You're too good for that. Too good for us.'

'Don't say that.'

'It's true.'

'It's not,' she says. 'Besides. It's too late. I've made up my mind. I've gotta go with her, Colt. No matter what happens from here, I'm with her.'

He sighs. 'I know. But I couldn't just say nothing.'

'Thank you, though,' she says. 'For worrying about me.'

'I warned you before. Dickinsons ain't easy to love.'

'It didn't stop me then, either.'

There's a long, heavy pause before Colt says, real quiet, 'I missed you, Agnes.'

Then they stop talking.

I turn my head and bury my face in the flat, smelly pillow.

Because the walls are real thin. And if I could hear them talking, then they might be able to hear me crying.

AGNES

'Sorry the party got broke up,' Bo said.

Colt had just dropped us off in my driveway. He'd also handed me my cane, which he'd managed to grab before we took off into the field.

'It's OK,' I said. 'I still had fun . . . Maybe more fun than I've ever had.'

I regretted saying it the second the words left my mouth. Damn it. Now Bo was gonna think I was a loser. Or some kind of hermit who never left the house and never had any fun. She'd never want to hang out with me again and—

'Good,' she said. 'I had more fun tonight than I usually have at these things.'

'Good.'

'Well,' she said, after a second. 'I better be getting home, I guess.'

114

There was something about the way she said it. Something tired. Or like there was a touch of dread in her voice. Like going home was the last thing she wanted.

I asked before I could stop myself. 'Do you wanna spend the night?' When she didn't answer immediately, I quickly added, 'I know that probably seems like a little-kid thing. Not even sure if people our age still have sleepovers. I mean I sleep over at Christy's on New Year's Eve every year, but that's different, so—'

'I'd love to,' Bo said.

'Really?'

'Agnes.' Mama's voice came from the front porch. 'Honey, why are y'all just standing out here?'

'We're just talking. Can Bo stay the night?'

'Oh . . . Um . . .'

It probably wasn't real nice to Mama, putting her on the spot again. But after today, I knew for sure that, no matter what she thought of her so far, Mama was way too polite to say no with Bo standing right there.

'Well, uh . . . sure. Of course,' she said. 'Y'all come on in. I'll make up a camp-bed for you, Bo.'

'You should probably call your mama and ask if it's OK,' I said as we made our way up the steps and through the front door.

'Nah. It's fine. She won't care.'

115

I tried not to react to that. I asked my parents' permission for almost everything. I wasn't even supposed to walk home from the bus stop alone. But Bo went to parties and stayed at friends' houses without even calling her mother. She went where she wanted, when she wanted.

I wondered what that sort of freedom felt like.

'How was the party?' Daddy asked after muting the ten o'clock news.

'Good,' I said. I was worried that if I said much more than that, I'd accidentally let it slip about the police being called. And there was no way my parents would take kindly to that.

'Really?' Daddy asked. 'Because you're home a little early. I thought maybe it ended up being kind of boring.'

I glanced over at Bo. 'No. Not boring at all.'

We headed upstairs to my bedroom. But just as we rounded the corner, I felt the heat of shame wash over me. Earlier, I'd been too focused on the party to worry about what Bo might think of my room. But now, staring at the yellow walls and the menagerie of stuffed animals, I saw it through Bo Dickinson's eyes. And it was humiliating. It was the bedroom of a little girl. Not a sixteen-year-old who'd just gone to a parentless, cop-busted party.

'Perfect timing,' Mama said when she noticed us in the doorway. 'I just finished the camp-bed. Hope it's comfortable, Bo. I can always get a couple extra blankets if you need them.'

'I'm sure it'll be great. Thank you, ma'am.'

'You're quite welcome. Let me know if y'all need anything else.'

'Thanks, Mama.'

'Thanks, ma'am.'

I shut the door behind Mama as she left the room. 'I'm sorry,' I said.

'What for?'

'My room. It's been this way since I was five . . . That's why it looks like a little girl's room.'

'I like it,' she said. 'I never really had a little girl's room. I was gonna ask this afternoon – are all those stuffed animals yours?'

'Yeah.'

'Do they all have names?'

'Of course not.' I laughed. But they did. All seventeen of them.

We turned on the TV and watched for a while before we both got tired. I lent her a pair of pyjamas even though they were way too big, but she didn't complain.

'Can we leave the TV on?' she asked after I shut off the

light. 'You can turn it down. I just . . . I sleep with it on at home.'

'Oh, sure,' I said. I'd never slept with the TV on before, but I was a heavy sleeper; sound never bothered me, and I didn't think the light from the screen would, either.

We lay there for a while, listening to an old episode of *The Andy Griffith Show* before Bo whispered, 'Agnes?'

'Yeah?'

'Tell me something.'

'What?'

'Anything. Tell me something I don't know about you.'

'Um . . .' I tried to think of something interesting. Something she'd find impressive. It was crazy. A few weeks ago, I didn't even like Bo Dickinson. Now I was constantly worried about making her like me. I was too tired to come up with anything good, though, so I said the first real thing I could think of. 'I really wanted to have a beer tonight.'

'Why didn't you?'

'I don't know. Chickened out, I guess. I've never drank before.'

'Never? Not even a sip?'

'Nope.'

I was worried she'd laugh or tease me, but she didn't. She stayed quiet.

118

'Your turn,' I said. 'Tell me something I don't know about you.'

'Well . . . I had a crush on Dana Hickman when we were in ninth grade.'

'Wait.' I rolled over to face her, even though it was too dark for me to see. 'You . . . like girls?'

'Boys, too.'

'Oh' was all I could say as I tried to wrap my head around what she'd just said.

'Is that . . . OK?'

'Yeah . . .' But I wasn't sure if it was or not. I'd grown up my whole life in the church, been told it was only all right for girls to like boys. Anything else was wrong. Then again, I'd been told being friends with a Dickinson was wrong, too. But I'd just had the best night of my life with Bo and Colt.

I didn't know how I felt about what Bo had just told me. But I did know, with great certainty, that I wanted to be her friend, whether it was wrong or not.

'Agnes?' she asked. 'What're you thinking? Are you mad?'

'No!' I said, real quick. 'Of course not. It's just . . .'

'Just what?'

'It's just . . . Dana Hickman? Bo, you have some awful taste.'

119

She burst out laughing. 'Don't I know it. In boys, too.'

'I wonder what else Dana would have said to us if Colt hadn't chased her off.'

'God only knows. She doesn't shut up when she's drinking.'

A few seconds later, our laughter died down and we fell silent again.

'Agnes?'

'Yeah?'

'I ain't told nobody that before,' she said. 'Not even Colt.'

'Why'd you tell me?'

'Dunno. I just . . . I felt like I could.'

I smiled, unable to hold back the joy her saying that gave me. Bo Dickinson had just shared something private with me, something she'd never told anyone else. It didn't matter how I felt about her secret. All that mattered was that I was the one she told.

I'd spent my whole life forced to trust others – trust them to guide me, to see for me – but no one had ever put that kind of trust in me. Not Christy. Not my sister. Not my parents.

Only Bo.

After a while, I whispered, 'Thank you.'

But she didn't answer, and I knew she'd already fallen asleep.

And, not too long after, I was, too.

She was gone when I woke up the next morning. The pyjamas I'd lent her were folded neatly on the camp-bed where she'd slept, and she'd turned the TV off before she'd gone.

I wasn't sure what to make of it. First I worried I'd done something wrong, that maybe she'd gotten upset with me and left. But then I remembered our whispered conversation the night before. Bo trusted me. I was special. Knowing that eased some of my worry, and I just figured maybe she had to go home. Maybe she had plans that day. I could ask her on Monday.

But Monday felt lifetimes away.

And before I could get to school and to Bo, I had to deal with church.

And Christy.

'I heard you were at Dana Hickman's party on Friday.' Christy had been waiting for me on the front steps, and after a few hellos, my parents had left us there. 'I heard you showed up with Bo Dickinson and her cousin. And that you danced with him. That can't be true, though, right?'

But by the way she asked, it was clear she knew well and good that it was.

Still, I had no clue what to say. I couldn't lie, and didn't want to. But if I confirmed, told her it was true, I knew she'd never let it go. I knew she'd grab my arm in that way she did, so tight it hurt, and tell me she was worried about me. And maybe she should be.

So I didn't say anything. Just nodded and started for the door of the sanctuary. It was almost time for Sunday school after all.

But Christy followed. She stuck close to me in the sanctuary, her hand grasping my upper arm, so anyone else might think she was guiding me. She wasn't, though. She was holding me back.

'What were you thinking?' she whispered, her mouth close to my ear, flecks of spit hitting my cheek.

'She invited me,' I said. 'And I wanted to go.'

'Why didn't you tell me? I'm your best friend, Agnes.'

I was surprised by how sad she sounded when she said this. Like I'd really hurt her. It wasn't the reaction I'd expected from the girl who told Dana Hickman I was clingy.

'You weren't at school,' I said. 'And I didn't think it mattered. You never invite me to parties.'

'Of course I haven't. Parties are dark and you're blind.

You wouldn't have fun anyway.'

It wasn't as if Christy had never said these things before. But for the first time, I felt a twinge of annoyance.

I was starting to realize that I'd spent years letting people tell me what I could and couldn't do, what I would and wouldn't enjoy because of my vision. And I let them because they were looking out for me. But since meeting Bo that day in the woods, my feelings had slowly begun to shift and tilt.

And after Friday night, going to a party, dancing in the grass, running through cornfields – things people would tell me I shouldn't or couldn't do – I didn't want people like Christy making those decisions for me anymore.

'Maybe you're right,' I said. 'Maybe I wouldn't have had fun with you. But I sure did with Bo.'

She gasped, about as surprised as I was that those words had just come out of my mouth. I'd never said anything like that to Christy. Never had the nerve. Even when I'd disagreed with her in the past, I mostly kept it to myself, scared of making her mad at me. Even now, I felt a weight settling on my chest, an old, anxious feeling I always got when I did something wrong.

Christy dropped my arm with a huff. 'Find your own way to the classroom,' she said before stomping off.

Despite my unease over what I'd said to her, I nearly laughed. I'd been going to this church since I was a baby. I could find my way around it in the dark without a cane, just like my own house, if I needed to. Getting to our Sunday school class without her wasn't a problem.

Unfortunately, the only seat left when I got to the room was the one right next to hers.

'Good morning, everyone,' Miss Kelly, our Sunday school teacher, said once I'd sat down. 'Let's get started with a prayer. Anyone have prayer requests today?'

'Can we pray for my aunt Georgia?' a younger boy, Eli, asked. 'We just found out she's got cancer.'

'I'm so sorry to hear that, Eli. We'll all pray for her. Anyone else?'

A few others requested prayers for friends and family members going through hard times. Then, I felt Christy's hand brush my shoulder as she raised it.

'Miss Kelly,' she said, using her sweet, candy-covered voice. 'I have a prayer request, too.'

The weight pressed harder on my chest as dread piled onto the anxiety.

'Of course, Christy. Go ahead.'

'I know there are some among us who might be struggling,' she said. 'Who've lost their way. Aligned themselves with sinners. I just pray for those people. I hope they can find their path again.'

My cheeks burned. She hadn't said my name, and I couldn't see anyone's faces just then, but I was sure everyone was looking at me. Sure they knew Christy meant I was the one aligning myself with sinners. And she was right. Bo Dickinson was a sinner if ever there was one. Between the fights and the boys and – after what she'd told me last night – the girls, too. Maybe I needed their prayers.

But, God help me, I didn't want them.

I took a deep breath, knowing I should just stay quiet. Bite my tongue.

'Well, all right,' Miss Kelly said, sounding a little confused. 'Sure. If that's everyone, let's join hands and—'

'Wait.'

I knew I ought to be quiet, but I was tired of doing what I ought to.

'Yes, Agnes?'

'I have a prayer request, too,' I said.

'Oh. OK. We have an awful lot today, it seems. Who do you want us to pray for?'

'I want to pray for people who eat shellfish,' I said.

'Excuse me?'

'Shellfish. According to the Bible, that's a sin.' I turned

to face Christy. She was staring right at me, so close that even I could tell she was scowling. 'Christy, didn't you say you and your boyfriend went to Red Lobster on a date not too long ago?'

'That's enough, Agnes,' Miss Kelly said.

But I was feeling mean now. I'd never been mean before, and it felt better than it ought to have.

'And didn't you get a haircut, too, Christy? I think that's also a sin, if I recall,' I said.

'Agnes!'

'And we've talked a whole lot about premarital sex being a sin, but just the other day, you—'

'That's it. Agnes Atwood, get out of my classroom,' Miss Kelly demanded.

'I'm just pointing out what the Bible says. If we're gonna talk about sinners . . .'

I glanced back at Christy, and I was surprised to realize that she wasn't scowling anymore. Her head was down, and I couldn't see her face. I did, however, hear a soft sniff.

'Go sit in the sanctuary until services start,' Miss Kelly said.

'Yes, ma'am.'

I stood up, unfolded my cane, and headed for the door, regret and guilt already starting to seep through

126

and put a damper on that meanness I'd revelled in a second before.

'You know, Agnes,' Christy said, and I thought I heard tears in her voice. 'You have fun with Bo Dickinson. Y'all might be perfect for each other.'

BO

'I think maybe I'm starting to like it,' Agnes says, running her fingers through her short hair.

I rinse my toothbrush and put it back in the plastic bag I'd packed it in. I move aside and Agnes steps in front of the sink, wetting the flannel she'd been given to wash her face. In the next room, I can hear Colt on the phone, but with the water running, I can't make out a word he's saying.

I pour some dog food into a bowl Colt had lent me and set it on the floor. Utah lunges at it, tail wagging. She don't know that it's the last of the food. That I'd been too anxious about getting out of the trailer the other night to think about how much I was packing.

'I think maybe it makes me look kinda badass.' She scrubs the rag along her nose and forehead. 'Like a rebel. Don't you think so?'

'Sure.'

She frowns in the mirror. 'You OK, Bo?'

I nod. Then, because I ain't sure she saw, I say, 'Fine. Just . . . tired. Didn't sleep too good.'

Agnes wrings out the flannel and sets it on the edge of the sink. She opens her mouth, like she's gonna say something, but in the next room, I hear Colt hang up the phone. I turn and yank the door open real fast.

'What'd he say?' I holler.

He don't answer, so I run out of the bathroom and down the short hall, to the kitchen. He's standing at the counter, looking tired and running his fingers through his hair.

'Well?' I ask.

'You owe me.' He sighs and shakes his head. 'He asked me for money. Can you believe that?'

''Course I can,' I say. 'You ain't gonna give it to him, though.'

'Got to. He made me promise I'd send him a hundred bucks. Was the only way he'd give me the address.'

'Jesus. Colt . . . I'm sorry.'

'Like I said. You owe me.' He rips a piece of paper out of the notepad next to the telephone, then he hands it to me. 'Here you go. Uncle Wayne's last known address. Dad ain't talked to him in a while, though, so who knows where he's at now.'

I look down at the address, but I ain't heard of the city or street. 'Any chance you got a map?' I ask.

He does. One of those big books of maps that people keep in their car on long trips. He bought it before he moved to this place, just in case he got turned around.

I sit down with the book open to the map of Kentucky, carefully looking at the names of every city and town.

'He's way out east,' I tell Colt and Agnes, who're sitting on the couch across from me. 'Out in the mountains.'

'That's a long drive,' Colt says.

I take a black marker and, real careful, trace the route from Colt's apartment to the street where Daddy lives. Or, where we think he lives. The thick black line is long and curvy, part highway, part city streets. Best I can figure, it'll take nearly four hours to get there. Longer if we hit traffic.

'Can I take this?' I ask, pointing to the map.

'Might as well,' Colt says. 'You done marked it up. It's yours now.'

'Thanks.'

'We'd better get going, then,' Agnes says, getting to her feet. 'Want me to take Utah out while you grab our stuff?'

'Uh . . . yeah. Sure.'

130

'There's a grassy area around the side of the building,' Colt tells her. 'Need me to help you find it?'

'That's all right. I've got my cane.' It takes her a second to find Utah's leash, but as soon as she picks it up, the dog runs right to her, ready for a morning pee.

Once they're out the door, Colt turns to me. 'You sure you wanna do this?' he asks.

'What other choice do I got?'

He don't answer. Because he knows there ain't no other choice. Not really. Going home's not an option now. All I can do is keep running.

After a second, he sighs. 'Fuck. There really ain't no winning here, is there?'

I shake my head. 'There never is for us.'

He almost smiles. Then he looks down at his bare feet on the carpet. 'Bo, you know I'd let you stay here, but—'

'I ain't gonna do that to you. You finally got out. Got away from all this. I already done enough damage making you call your dad. I can't drag you down no more.'

He looks up, and I wonder if he recognizes the words I just used. Repeating back what he said to Agnes last night. But if he does, he don't show it. 'I wanted to get you out of there, too,' he says. 'It's always been my plan, you know. To get settled in and . . . I dunno. Save some money so I could get you out of Mursey, too. Get you away from all that.'

'Well, this is my way of doing it myself. Might not be the best way, but I don't got another choice.'

He looks like he might argue, but the door opens and Agnes comes back in with Utah.

'All right,' she says. 'Are we ready?'

I stand up and tuck the book of maps under my arm. I grab our bags and head toward the front door.

Colt follows me. He gives Agnes a hug that lasts a second too long, and I see her whisper something in his ear. After he lets her go, Colt turns to me. He puts his arms around me and pulls me in, and I damn near start to cry. He holds me tight, tighter than he has before. I know he's worried, and I hate it. I don't wanna hurt him. Since I can remember, Colt's been the only person I've ever really loved. The only one who's loved me back.

Until Agnes.

'Be careful,' he whispers.

Then, slowly, he lets go.

Outside, in the parking lot, Agnes uses her cane to find her way to the passenger's side of the Reliant K. 'So we're going almost all the way across the state, right? Think there will be any cool things to see along the way? How far are we gonna be from Cumberland Falls?'

I stop at the driver's-side door, Utah's leash in one hand, car keys in the other.

When I don't move for a second, she asks, 'Are you gonna open the door?'

'Listen, Agnes . . . You ain't gotta come with me if you don't want. It's a long drive, and I'm sure Colt'll take you back to Mursey if you want him to. I won't be mad if you don't come, so—'

'What're you talking about?' she asks, staring at me over the roof of the car. 'Of course I'm coming. Don't you want me to?'

'Yeah, I do.'

More than anything. The idea of going alone scares the shit out of me. But I gotta give her an out. I'm a good enough person to do that.

'Well, then, unlock the car,' she says. 'Because you and me have a long way to go.'

'OK.' I unlock the car and watch her climb inside.

Because I'm a good enough person to give her an out, but I ain't good enough to make her take it.

AGNES

Bo wasn't at school on Monday. At least, I couldn't find her. I searched, looking for a glimpse of that red-gold hair. I listened, hoping to hear her voice in the halls. But instead, all I heard were the whispers.

Word had gotten out about what I'd said in Sunday school class, which wasn't surprising considering who I'd said it to. In all the years I'd known Christy, I'd never known her to keep gossip to herself. Especially if it might get her any kind of sympathy. I was worried everyone would be mad at me. And maybe some people were. But some were . . . impressed.

'Is it true?' Dana Hickman asked when she found me in the library, sitting alone with my history book and a magnifier during lunch. 'Did you really tell Christy she was going to hell in the middle of church?'

'Um . . . I guess. Something like that.'

'Damn, Agnes,' she said. 'And partying with Dickinsons on Friday? Didn't think you had it in you.'

She wasn't the only one who felt that way, apparently. A few others said the same thing throughout the day. Even Andrew brought it up when I ran into him out in the parking lot after school, while I was waiting for Mama to come pick me up.

'You're not the girl I thought you were, Agnes.'

It didn't seem likely he meant that as a compliment, all things considered, but it felt like one. You don't realize how much people underestimate you until they start . . . estimating you. For the first time, the people at school weren't seeing me as Agnes, the poor, sweet little blind girl.

And I wasn't seeing myself that way, either.

When Mama and I got home, I decided to do my homework on the front porch. It was so nice outside, just slightly cool and not humid at all. Perfect early-autumn weather. And the house felt stifling. It wasn't sudden. It had been creeping up on me for a while, this feeling of being caged. But you don't always know something is choking you until it's already too tight and you can't breathe real well. That's what the house felt like now.

So I took one of my special notebooks – one of the

ones full of paper that had lines so thick and dark that even I could see where I ought to write. Lines on regular notebook paper were too thin, too light, and I always ended up with sentences that sloped down the page like wilting flowers.

But with my special paper and a felt-tip pen, I could usually write an essay that was at least somewhat legible. Today's essay was for English, a line-by-line analysis of a poem of my choosing. Considering Bo had been on my mind all day, it wasn't a surprise I'd chosen something by Emily Dickinson.

I uncapped my pen and wrote the first couple lines.

Behind Me – dips Eternity –
Before Me – Immortality –

I stopped and tapped my chin with my pen, thinking of what to write, what my analysis of these words were. I wondered what Bo's thoughts on the poem would be.

And then, like that thought had conjured her, she was there.

There was a car with a loud engine idling in front of our driveway, but I didn't think much of it until I heard her voice, shouting my name out the window.

'Agnes!'

I didn't have to look up. My heart started beating real fast, but, at the same time, I felt relieved. The way you feel when you finally get to take your bra off at the end of the day.

'Come on,' she said. 'Let's go for a ride.'

'Who's car do you have?' I hollered back.

'Stole it.' I must have looked horrified, even all the way across the yard. 'Jesus, I'm kidding. It's my mama's. And she knows I got it . . . Or, she will when she wakes up. But that ain't gonna be for a while, I reckon. So come on.'

I glanced at my front door. Mama had complained of a headache when we got home this afternoon, and she'd gone to lie down. And nobody wanted to wake Mama up when she had a headache. Not if they wanted to keep their own head intact.

'Where would we be going?' I asked.

'Nowhere far.'

I knew I ought to tell Mama where I was going. She might be mad if she woke up and I was gone. But she'd also be mad if I woke her up for anything short of an emergency. And Gracie used to go out after school all the time with her friends. No one even expected her home until dinner.

But I'd never gone out after school before. Not on a

weeknight. I stayed home. Every day. Every night.

'Agnes?' Bo called. 'You coming or what?'

I looked down at my notebook and the black, scratchy writing there.

> *Behind Me – dips Eternity –*
> *Before Me – Immortality –*

I flipped the page, tore out a blank sheet, and scribbled a quick note to Mama. I ran inside, left the note on the counter, and grabbed my cane.

'Ready?' Bo asked when I hopped down the front steps and moved toward the car.

'Ready,' I answered.

And I climbed inside, eager to see what lay before me.

'Wow. Bet Christy didn't like that too well,' she said when I told her the Sunday school story in the car.

'Nope. She's already told everyone in school. It's funny, though. Some people are mad at me, sure. But most people, I think, were just surprised. They can't believe I said it.'

'How come?'

'Well . . . partly because she's my best friend.'

Or was she?

I hadn't even questioned it until just then. But it seemed almost impossible that we could keep being best friends now. And, despite everything, I felt a pang of sadness at the realization. We'd been close for years. Since we were little. She'd been my first – my only – best friend. And while I wasn't sure exactly how things would change in the long run, I knew they had to. I couldn't imagine us just going back to sitting together at lunch and talking on the church steps on Sundays.

But as sad and uncertain as I felt about my friendship with Christy, I was also excited. Because Bo and I were spending more time together, and whenever we did, it was like a shot of adrenaline. A combination of anticipation and relief, an overwhelming need to spend every second with her.

I couldn't remember ever feeling that way with Christy.

'And also,' I continued, 'I don't know. I don't think people expect that out of me. Everybody sees me as this sweet, innocent blind girl.'

'What the hell does blind got to do with it?' Bo asked as we turned onto a gravel road. I still wasn't sure where we were going.

'I mean . . . it doesn't, I guess.'

139

Or maybe it did. I always got the feeling that was why people thought of me as sweet and innocent. Because I was blind. In stories, the injured, the weak, they were always good. Kind and innocent. More than once, I'd heard the women at my church describe me as 'an angel'. They'd tell Mama that God only sent angels like me to parents he knew could handle the challenge. I was a precious gift to be taken care of.

But I wasn't an angel. I was just a kid who couldn't see real well.

'I don't think of you that way,' Bo said.

'You don't?'

'As a sweet, innocent blind girl? Nah. I mean, you're nice and all. But you're tough, too. I think you're kind of a badass.'

I laughed. Because there was no way that was true, no matter how much I wanted it to be. Telling off Christy was the only badass thing I'd done in my life. And even that had made me feel bad.

Bo didn't laugh, though. 'I ain't kidding,' she said. 'I think you're a Loretta.'

'What?'

'Loretta Lynn,' she said. 'She's nice – at least, I like to think she is – but she's tough, too. She dealt with a lotta shit, but she just keeps going. You're a Loretta.'

140

'I don't know,' I said. 'I always related more to Tammy Wynette.'

'Fuck that,' Bo said. 'Tammy's all right, but she ain't got a backbone. She stands by her man. She's a good girl, but she only goes bad to impress a guy. That ain't you. You're a Loretta.'

I still thought she was wrong, but I didn't argue. Instead, I asked, 'And who are you?'

'Me?' She sighed. 'I'm a Patsy.'

Patsy Cline. I sat there in the passenger's seat, trying to think of her reasoning behind this. To me, Bo seemed more like a Loretta. She was loud and didn't take crap from anybody. But Patsy . . . was so sad. Her songs were about missing people, being lonely, yearning. I wanted to ask her why. Why Patsy? But, somehow, that silly question felt almost too personal.

Besides, the car was slowing down. I stared out the window, wondering where we were, but all I could see were trees and, straight ahead of us—

'Are we at the river?'

'Sure are.' Bo cut the engine and climbed out of the car.

I didn't know what to do at first. I wasn't sure why we'd just gone to the river. There was nothing to do here. Nothing interesting. It was the river that separated

Mursey from the next town over. We'd all been there. All fished on it. There was no reason to go there if you didn't have a boat and some live bait.

But Bo was getting something out of the trunk, so I climbed out of the car and just stood there, next to the door.

'I got you something,' she said, shutting the trunk.

'What?'

She walked over to me and held out the thing she'd gotten from the trunk. I reached out, my eyes not really processing it as more than a box. But then I understood.

'Beer?'

'You said you wanted to try one,' she said. 'Here's twelve. But drinking them all at once probably ain't such a good idea.'

'Where did you get these?' I asked.

'My fridge. They're Mama's. She ain't gonna miss them. I'll just tell her one of her boyfriends drank them.'

We sat on the hood of the car, our backs pressed to the windshield as I popped open my first beer. Bo hadn't taken one, probably because she was driving. And, even though I didn't know much about alcohol, I knew for someone as tiny as Bo, it probably wouldn't take much to get drunk.

I sniffed the open can. The odour was strong and familiar. One I'd smelled a million times on hot days when Daddy opened a cold can before watching a ball game. Part of me was still nervous, still worried about breaking the rules. But it didn't seem as scary drinking with just Bo. It felt safer than the party. And, she'd just told me I was a badass.

Slowly, I lifted the can to my lips and took a sip.

And gagged.

'Ugh.'

'No good?' Bo asked.

'It's kinda what I'd imagine pee tastes like,' I said. 'Why do people drink it?'

'Guess they ain't too worried about the taste.'

'It's awful.'

But I took another sip. And another.

'How come you weren't at school today?' I asked.

'Dunno. Didn't feel like it.'

'Oh.'

She said it so casually. Like this was a choice she got to make every day. She'd wake up in the morning and choose whether she wanted to eat cereal or Pop-Tarts, to wear the pink shirt or the blue, to go to school or to not. Bo didn't seem to have any rules. She could spend the night without asking permission, take her mama's

143

car, and basically do whatever she wanted. No one seemed to care.

Well, not no one. In a way, I guess everyone cared. What with the whole town keeping an eye on Bo and all. Judging her for every little thing she did. And even some things she didn't do.

Still, Bo was free.

'Tell me something I don't know about you,' she said. It was the same thing she'd said Friday night in my bedroom, when I'd told her I'd wanted to have a drink at the party.

I took another sip of the beer. A longer one this time. The taste was still bad, but it didn't make me gag. 'Um . . . Well . . .'

Once again, I was having a hard time thinking of anything cool or interesting. But I remembered Bo's answer last time. The secret she'd told me. She hadn't tried to impress me. She'd just been honest.

'I've never kissed anyone,' I said finally.

She didn't laugh. Or say 'Awww.' Or try and make me feel better about it. She just asked, 'Is there somebody you wanna be kissing?'

'Maybe . . .'

Truth was, I'd been thinking about Colt a lot since the party and that dance. The night before, I'd laid in bed remembering the way his hands felt on me and trying to imagine what it would feel like to kiss him. Then I'd just rolled over and tried to push the thought out of my head. Colt Dickinson was moving away soon. He wouldn't be interested in kissing a high school girl. Especially not me. And, even if he were, he was still Colt Dickinson. He wasn't the kind of boy you had a first kiss with.

I didn't wanna tell Bo any of that, though. I wasn't sure how she'd feel about me thinking of her cousin that way. Probably that I was crazy. Or desperate. I'd danced with the boy once, and now I was wanting to kiss him?

So before she could ask who I was maybe wanting to kiss, I said, 'Now you. Tell me something I don't know about you.'

'All right . . . It's stupid and it's pointless and it ain't never gonna happen but . . . I wanna be a country singer.'

'You sing?' I asked.

'Sometimes.'

I took another drink of the beer. Then, because I was feeling bolder than I usually did, I said, 'Sing something for me. Now.'

Bo just laughed.

'I'm serious,' I said. 'I wanna hear you sing.'

'I don't sing in front of people.'

'You're never gonna make it as a country singer, then.'

'You're right. I won't.'

'Come on, Bo. Please? Just a little bit of a song?'

She sighed. Then, so quiet I couldn't make out the words, she sang. But with each note, each lyric, she got a little louder. Until I finally recognized the song.

"'Jolene, Jolene,'" she sang, her voice getting louder and clearer.

And she could sing. Real well. Her voice was rich and thick. And it even had a little bit of Dolly Parton's vibrato.

By the time she hit the chorus again, she'd gotten past whatever nerves had kept her from singing in front of people before. Like the music was in her, like it had possessed her, she hopped to her feet, standing on the hood of the car. Then she climbed onto the roof.

I spun around to watch as she belted out the song, using the roof as her stage. Her feet tapped to the beat and her arms waved around. I smiled. I couldn't help it. No one who saw this could think of Bo Dickinson as anything but wonderful.

I finished my beer and tossed the can on the ground, making a note to pick it up later. Bo had finished 'Jolene' and started in on 'Delta Dawn' already, and that feeling that had dragged her onto the roof of the car found its

146

way into me, too, because I started singing along with my not-so-nice voice.

"'And did I hear you say, he was a-meeting you here today . . .'"

And then, without thinking, I was standing up on the hood, trying to keep my balance and the tune as I moved to join her on the roof. I stumbled a little, and Bo grabbed my hand.

For a second, we both stopped singing.

I thought she'd tell me to be careful. Tell me getting on the roof was a bad idea. I might fall. I couldn't see the edge. She wouldn't have been wrong.

But she reached for my other hand and pulled me up to join her. To share her stage.

She started singing again, picking up from where we left off.

We sang our way through half a dozen songs like that, belting them out from the roof of the car. And even though I almost lost my balance a few times, Bo never told me to get down. She just kept her hands close. Not gripping, not clinging. Just close. Ready to catch me if I started to fall.

BO

'Hey, it's our song.' Agnes leans forward and turns up the Reliant K's radio. '"Laugh with me, buddy,"' she sings along with Willie Nelson, smiling at me. She's wanting me to sing, too.

I can't, though.

I try to smile back, but the corners of my mouth feel heavy, and I'm glad she can't see my face real well. 'Since when is this our song?'

She stops singing for a second to answer. 'Since I decided just now.'

We've been in the car for about an hour, and she's been talking and singing the whole time, acting like we're on a road trip instead of running from the law.

'Maybe we could get a cat,' she says once the song is over.

'What?'

'A cat. In our new place. Do you think Utah would get along with a cat?'

'I . . . I dunno.'

'Let's ask.' She turns in her seat, looking back at the dog. 'What do you think, Utah? Should we get a kitten when we find a place of our own?'

I hear Utah's tail thumping against the backseat.

'You gotta promise not to eat the cat, though,' Agnes says. 'Can you promise that?'

The tail keeps thumping.

'Good.' Agnes spins back around in her seat, laughing and smiling in a way that oughta make me feel happy but instead makes my chest ache. 'Utah promises not to eat our future pet cat. So it's decided.'

I keep my eyes on the stretch of blacktop ahead, trying hard to fight the thoughts of me and Agnes in an apartment with Utah and a cat. In my imagination, it's small and white and way too fluffy. And she's named it something like Waylon or Hank, after a country music singer. And we've got a place that's small but clean, with bookshelves full of poetry and braille books and a kitchen that ain't never empty.

I fight it because as nice as it sounds, that ain't what's gonna happen.

But I can't tell her that. Not yet.

'Hey, listen,' Agnes says after a minute. 'I've been thinking. I know we're headed out to your daddy's, and it's a long ride. But we're not in a big hurry, are we?'

I glance at her, then look back at the road. 'Depends how you look at it. Why?'

'I was just thinking . . . I've never been outside of Mursey, and no one but Colt knows what car we're driving now . . . We ought to make the most of this driving, you know? Make a few stops. Have a little fun.'

So she does think we're on a road trip.

'Agnes, we don't got much money—'

'I know,' she says. 'And we don't have to spend it, either. I'm not talking about tourist-type stuff, I just . . . If we see anything that seems fun, let's try and actually stop, OK? Just to check it out. We might not get to your daddy's until tomorrow, but that's all right. What do you think?'

I oughta say no. I oughta keep driving and get out east, into the mountains, as fast as I can. The police are looking for us, and a couple bad haircuts and a cheap-bought car ain't gonna disguise us for long.

But when I look at her again, out of the corner of my eye, she's just smiling at me. Her hair's blowing around in the wind, and she looks beautiful and hopeful. And I realize, even though she doesn't, that we probably

150

won't get this chance again. If we don't take the time to have some fun now, there's a good chance we never will.

And I want her to have at least one good memory of me when all this is said and done.

'All right,' I say. 'You spot anything that seems fun, we'll make a stop.'

'Yes!' she shouts, and she sounds so much like a little girl that even I gotta laugh through the ache in my stomach and the tightness in my throat. 'But you'll have to do the spotting, Bo. It's not really my strong suit.'

I smile. 'All right. I'll keep an eye out.'

And it don't gotta be out long before I see something.

We're driving through a little town, no bigger than Mursey, when I spot a sign taped in the window of some restaurant as we pass.

SUMMER STREET FAIR!!
EVERY NIGHT THIS WEEK
MAPLE AVENUE, 7–11 P.M.
LIVE MUSIC! GOOD BARBECUE!

I slow the car down as we pass, reading the large block letters.

This town's tiny enough that it ain't likely any cops

would be looking for us here. And if the street fair gets crowded – and since it's only one street, it might – it'd be easy to take off and disappear if anybody did recognize us. It's a little risky, but maybe not too bad.

And it could be fun, I reckon.

A couple years back, the week Colt turned sixteen and bought that old pickup truck he'd been saving lawn-mowing and tobacco-field money for since he was ten, he'd taken me to a town half an hour down the road and we'd found ourselves at one of these summer street fairs. We'd wandered around for hours, listening to the band and smiling at strangers who didn't know us as town trash.

We'd danced and laughed and a cute boy had even given me his phone number. Not because he thought I'd blow him in someone's hayloft, either. Just because he thought I was pretty.

I'd never called, but it still felt real good.

And every now and then Colt and I talked about going back to that street fair. We never made it out there, though. Something else always came up. But I still think about it. About how nice it felt to have fun with strangers who didn't know my name, didn't know my story.

Didn't know what a horrible, lying bitch I was.

I am.

'Bo?' Agnes asks. 'Why'd you slow down? What's going on?'

'Nothing,' I say, swallowing hard. I turn to look at her and try to smile, even though it hurts. 'You up for some barbecue tonight?'

AGNES

'Where the hell have you been?'

It was the first thing I heard when I walked through my front door. Bo had just dropped me off after spending a couple hours down by the river. And in the couple hours, apparently, Mama had gotten up and Daddy had come home.

And they were furious.

'I . . . was with Bo,' I said. 'I left a note. Didn't you see it?'

'We were worried sick,' Mama said. She was standing in front of the couch. Like she was just too angry to entertain the idea of sitting down. 'I woke up and you were gone, and you hadn't taken your phone with you. I was on the verge of calling the cops.'

'I was just down the road,' I told her. 'At the river. What's the big deal?'

'The big deal? The big deal?'

'Honey,' Daddy said from his seat in the recliner. His voice was a lot calmer than Mama's. It almost always was. 'Your mother and I are a little worried about you. We heard about your outburst in church the other day. Christy's parents told us. Christy was real upset about something you said to her. And that just . . . It doesn't seem like you.'

'And now you're taking off without warning.' Mama sounded like she was teetering on the edge between fury and heartache. I couldn't tell if the cracks in her words were tears or barely held-back rage. Or both. 'And going to parties? Is this because of Bo Dickinson?'

'What? No.'

Although, I guess, it sort of was.

'I don't understand,' I said, twisting my cane in my hands. 'I'm sorry I forgot my phone, but I left a note. I told you I'd be back soon.'

'You think a note is enough?' Mama demanded. 'You didn't say where you were going. We didn't have a way to check on you if we needed to. You could've gotten hurt or lost or—'

'I was with Bo,' I said. 'I told you—'

'We barely know Bo, sweetheart,' Daddy said. 'We don't know yet how much we can trust her with you.'

I frowned. Trust her with me. I knew what that meant. He didn't know how well he could trust her to take care of me. To babysit me. Was that how he saw my friendship with Christy, too? Had she just been my responsible babysitter?

'You know her better than you knew a lot of Gracie's friends,' I pointed out, trying to keep my voice calm. 'And she was allowed to go out with them after school. You didn't always know where she was, but—'

'That's different,' Mama said.

'How?'

I knew the answer. I'd have to be a fool not to. But I wanted to hear it from them.

They didn't respond, though. Instead, Mama ignored me. 'You haven't been acting like yourself,' she said. 'And your father and I think—'

'How?!' And this time, I didn't bother to keep my voice down. That same anger that had filled me the other day in church was back, but without the hint of meanness. And for the first time in my life, I was back-talking my parents. 'How am I different from Gracie? How?!'

I didn't have to see their faces real well to know they were both shell-shocked. Gracie was the one who yelled, not me. Never me.

Until today, at least.

And they didn't even know about the beer.

Daddy was the one to recover. And this time, he was the one to do something he'd never done before. In a voice quiet as a snake's hiss he said, 'You're grounded. For a month. You go to school. You come home. And that's it.'

'Daddy—'

'That's. It.'

And no matter how mad I was, I knew better than to question him anymore.

'How much longer you grounded for?' Bo asked.

'Eight days.'

In the three weeks since my parents had locked me up, the season had fully changed. It was early October, and the wind was getting cold.

I'd been worried, at first, that my new friendship with Bo would blow away, fall like one of the leaves on our maple trees, while I was trapped in my house. But she'd surprised me. Bo had been at school every day. And even though she never said so, I liked to believe it was because she wanted to see me. We ate lunch together, walked together in the hallways, and even managed to get seats next to each other in English. Which was great, since Bo understood poetry so much better than I did.

There were lots of rumours going around about me. Some people thought I must've gone crazy. Others called me a slut. Not because of anything I'd done. Just because when it came to the Dickinsons, all their friends were guilty by association. But Bo seemed more bothered by what people were saying about me than I was. For me, none of it mattered as long as I got to spend every free minute of the school day with her.

And then, when I got home, I only had to wait an hour or so before Bo would call me. My parents hadn't made any rules about the phone, so I'd sit at the kitchen counter, doing homework, and waiting for the ring.

Sometimes we'd talk about a million things, and sometimes we'd just sit with the phones pressed to our ears, not saying much as we did our homework together.

'Fuck,' Bo said. 'I feel like you've been grounded forever.'

'Me too.'

'Colt was asking about you the other day.'

I sat up straighter. 'He was?' I glanced toward the sink, where Mama was washing dishes. Then I lowered my voice. 'What . . . what did he say?'

'Nothing much. Just asked where you were. Told me to say hi.'

'Oh. Well . . . That's nice. Tell him hello for me, too.'

'In eight days, you can tell him yourself,' she said. 'Also, Colt and me were talking, and I think the three of us oughta take a road trip down to Tennessee. What do you think? We could go to Nashville. Just take off for a few weeks. What do you think?'

I thought she was crazy. My folks grounded me for going down the street without proper permission. They'd never let me leave the state. Not with Bo Dickinson or anyone else. But I didn't want to say that to her. Didn't want her to get bored of me when I was so close to being released.

So I just said, 'Yeah. Maybe.'

'Agnes.' Mama had turned around from her spot at the sink and was looking my way now. 'Only fifteen more minutes on the phone. Then I want your help making dinner.'

'Yes, ma'am.'

I didn't think Mama was real happy about me talking to Bo every day. She never came out and told me not to, but I could tell she was still mad at Bo for taking me down to the river. Every time I got off the phone, she'd make a point of asking why I didn't call Christy more often.

When she'd left the kitchen, I pressed the phone back

to my ear, just in time to hear Bo say, 'Tell me something I don't know about you.'

I smiled. 'All right. I . . . really, really hate cooking.'

Bo laughed.

'Mama always wants me to help her. And I do, but I hate it. And not because I can't see real well so it's hard. I hate it because you spend all this time making something and half the time eating it. It drives me crazy.' I sighed. 'Just another reason nobody's gonna want to marry me, and I'll be stuck in my parents' house forever.'

'Oh, bullshit. You ain't gonna have any trouble finding someone to marry you. I think the hard part's gonna be finding someone you wanna marry. Ain't nobody in this town good enough for you.'

I felt myself blushing. It was insane, of course. There wasn't exactly a line of boys banging down the door for a chubby blind girl who didn't like to cook. But the fact that Bo thought that way about me, that the boys in Mursey didn't deserve me, it felt real good.

'Your turn,' I said. 'Tell me something I don't know about you.'

'I . . . One time I punched Nolan Curtis in the face.'

'That doesn't count,' I said. 'Because I knew that. Everybody knows that.'

Bo sighed. 'Fine. All right . . . Um . . . I . . .' She hesitated, then swallowed, so loud I heard it through the receiver. 'Sometimes, I miss my daddy.'

I was quiet for a second, because I wasn't quite sure what to say to this. Bo hadn't told me a whole lot about her parents. I got the sense that she didn't like talking about them much. So all I knew was that her mama did meth and her daddy had left when she was young. Other than that, she'd never seemed real comfortable sharing much about them.

'Everybody in town thinks he's this awful guy,' she continued. 'But he ain't so bad. Or, at least, he wasn't when I knew him. Sure, he drank a little too much and he broke some laws, but . . . we used to cook together, speaking of. Mama don't cook, but Daddy used to. All the time. And he always let me help him. He'd pull a chair into the kitchen so I could stand on it and reach the counter. Then I'd help him mash the potatoes or . . . sorry. It's probably stupid. I just miss shit like that sometimes.'

'It's not stupid at all,' I said. 'And . . . I know it's not the same, but if you ever wanna come over and cook with my mama, I'm sure she'd like that.'

Bo snorted. 'Yeah, right. Your folks probably hate me.'

'No, they don't,' I said. 'They just don't know you real

well. If they hated you, they wouldn't let me talk to you like this every day . . . And I bet Mama would like you a whole lot if you did cook with her. I'm sure you're more help than me. I'm just saying, if you ever wanted to . . .'

Bo was quiet for a second before, in a soft voice, she repeated my earlier words back to me. 'Yeah . . . maybe.'

BO

We wander around the tiny town for a few hours before heading over to Maple Avenue around seven. The street's blocked off, so no cars can drive down, and there are tables covered by little white tents all up the sidewalk. Some of them are selling food – the promised barbecue, some lemonade – and others are just cool, shady places for folks to sit until the sun has gone down.

In the middle of it all, there's an open trailer, set up like a stage, and a few guys with guitars are strumming chords and checking speakers there.

It's early, but there are already plenty of people out, greeting each other in the street and filling paper plates with food. Agnes and me ain't got much money, but we spend a little of the cash on some barbecue chicken that we split with Utah.

By the time we finish eating, the band's done started.

They're playing covers of country songs. Upbeat stuff all about honky-tonks and good-looking girls. And there's a crowd around the stage, people singing along and dancing.

'We should dance,' Agnes says.

I laugh, thinking she's kidding at first.

'I'm serious,' she says. 'You said we were gonna have fun. Dancing is fun.'

'I don't dance,' I tell her.

'But you will,' she says. 'You know how I know? Because you're Bo Dickinson, and you'll do anything for me. And all I'm asking for is to dance.'

I sigh.

'Come on,' she whines. 'These people don't know us. Who cares if we embarrass ourselves? We'll be gone tomorrow.'

She's smiling at me. Grinning, really. And I remind myself again that this might be our last shot at a good time. And I want Agnes to remember me at my best. As the kind of friend who gave her her first beer, who shared secrets in her dark bedroom, who danced with her at a street fair in a town we didn't even know the name of.

'Fine,' I say, standing up from the picnic table we've been sitting at for the past hour. I tether Utah's leash to the table leg and take Agnes by the arm as she folds up her cane and drops it on the bench.

'Guard it, Utah,' she tells the dog, who's too busy looking for scraps on the ground to even look up.

I guide her out toward the stage, into the crowd. The minute I let go of her arm, she grabs my hand and spins me around like a ballerina in a music box. And I can't help laughing.

'Told you dancing was fun.' She only sounds a little smug.

I try to spin her back, but I can't get my arm over her head, so Agnes has to duck as she turns, which sets us both into fits.

We dance like this for a while, neither of us leading or following. Sometimes we just keep turning each other. Sometimes we try and do moves we learned in elementary school, when they made us square dance. We hook elbows and trot in a circle, our feet in rhythm with the banjo that's playing onstage.

And for a second it's so perfect that I forget where we are and what's happened over the last few days. I forget where we're going and everything that I know's about to come.

It's just me and Agnes and her laugh and this song and nothing else.

At least until the song stops.

Then I remember again.

'You OK?' Agnes asks, a little breathless.

'Yeah . . . just . . . told you I don't dance.'

'All right, all right. Let's go sit down. I'm sure Utah's wondering what the heck we're doing anyway.'

A smile. 'Poor dog thinks we've gone crazy.'

'Oh, I'm thinking that bridge was burned a while ago, Bo.'

'That dog had to live with my mama. I doubt much fazes her at this point.' We get to the table, and I hand Agnes her folded cane. 'Wanna walk around some? I'm thinking we oughta spare a buck for some lemonade.'

'Sure.'

I'm bent down, untying Utah from the table, when I hear him. Or maybe I smell him first. It's the smell of beer and sweat. And it's right behind us.

'You looked sexy out there.'

I stand up and turn to see a skinny, shirtless guy. He's wearing cutoff shorts and holding an open beer bottle in his hand. I ain't sure how old he is, but he's too old to be looking at Agnes with that gross glint in his eye, that's for damn sure.

Agnes just ignores him. She might not even know he's talking to her. She unfolds her cane and looks at me.

'Hey. You hear me?' he asks, slurring his words together. 'I liked watching you dance. Why don't you come over here so I can get a better look at that ass?'

Now Agnes knows he's talking to her. She looks at him, and right when I'm about to go for his throat, she says, 'Fuck off.'

I grin at her. It's the first time I've really heard her stand up for herself. Not that I'm surprised. I've always known that she's tough, even if she don't see it. I offer her my arm and she loops hers through it. We ain't even taken two steps, though, when the prick yells after us.

'Have it your way, fat bitch.'

I spin around so fast that Agnes, holding on to my arm, stumbles.

'What the hell did you just call her?' I demand.

'I said she's a fucking fat bitch.'

I don't know I'm gonna hit him until we're already toppling to the pavement and my fist has slammed into his nose. But I guess that's how almost all my fights are. One minute I'm standing still and the next I'm throwing punches. But no matter how they start, I always win.

I hear Utah barking and Agnes yelling my name. Hear people in the crowd shouting. But all I can think about is the blood coming from this guy's nose and where I'm gonna hit next.

But even though he's skinny, he's taller than me and probably a good thirty or forty pounds heavier. So after I get a few good punches and kicks in, he gets his senses together and shoves me on my back. My head hits the concrete, and for a minute I see stars. But I still manage to slam my knee up into his crotch. He grunts in pain, but he don't let me up. Instead, he throws his own punch, right in my eye.

'Get the fuck off her!'

I just barely see the long white cane flying down and colliding with the back of this asshole's neck.

He yelps and jumps up, but I'm guessing he's more surprised than hurt. Either way, it gives me a chance to throw my weight – little as it is – at him, knock him back on the ground. I throw another punch and land it right on his mouth.

I might have a black eye, but he's gonna be missing a tooth.

Then there are hands on my shoulders – lots of them – dragging me off the motherfucker. And there are hands on him, too, pulling him away, across the pavement.

A few people ask me if I'm all right. Others ask me what the hell is wrong with me and call me a crazy bitch. And someone else shoves a ziplock bag full of ice in my hand, tells me to put it on my eye.

'Bo,' Agnes says, at my shoulder. She's got her cane in one hand and Utah's leash in the other. 'Oh my God. What were you thinking? I mean, thank you. But what the hell were you thinking?'

I ain't got a chance to answer before someone shouts, 'Cops are on their way.'

'Oh shit,' I say. 'Agnes.'

But she heard it, too, and shoves Utah's leash into my hand before taking hold of my arm.

I push through the crowd, avoiding hands that try to grab me, to hold us back. We dodge in and out of the crowd as strangers yell after us, telling us to stay, to stop.

But we can't do that. Because we cannot be here when the cops come.

So we run.

AGNES

After my grounding was over, Bo and I became inseparable. Not just at school, but everywhere. She spent nearly every Friday night at my house, and she must've been growing on my parents, because when she wasn't around, they asked after her. How she was doing in school, if she'd taught Utah any new tricks, that sort of thing. Mama even asked once what she liked to eat so that we could have one of her favourite meals for dinner when she came over next.

But Daddy was the one who'd really taken to her. Probably because she laughed at his jokes more often than Mama and I did, and he loved talking to her about Utah, who camped out on our back porch whenever Bo was over. It was more than that, though. He even defended her when Grandma made a comment about rumours that I was spending time with 'that harlot'.

Daddy stood up for Bo real fast.

'She's a nice girl,' he told Grandma. 'And it's sure hard to imagine she's doing all the running around people seem to say when she's at our dinner table most nights.'

I gave Daddy so many hugs in the days after that, he must've thought I'd lost my mind.

Daddy was also the one who convinced Mama to let me go out with Bo sometimes. Not to parties. They always had an excuse why that wasn't all right. But sometimes they'd let us go grab some fries and a milkshake at Marty's, a little fast-food place down the road. Colt almost always met us there, but we didn't tell my folks about that. They may have liked Bo, but I wasn't sure they could handle me spending so much time with a male Dickinson.

But the more time I spent with Colt, the more I realized how wrong people were about him. He was quieter than Bo, but obviously very protective of her. He seemed more like her brother than her cousin. And when he smiled at me – a smile so wide even I could see – it gave me this fluttering feeling in my stomach.

And sometimes, just occasionally, when our legs would brush under the table or he'd touch my shoulder for an instant – it made me think again about what it might feel like to kiss him. And I knew I was gonna be sad when he left for his new job in January.

Not that I'd told Bo that, though. It was one of the few secrets I kept.

'Tell me something I don't know about you' had become our little game. We played almost every time we were alone together, and I devoured each detail I learned about Bo.

Like that her full name was Isabo June Dickinson.

Or that she was deathly allergic to bees and, because of that, was terrified of them.

Or how when she was eleven, her mama brought home a German shepherd puppy without any warning. She'd bought the dog from a guy in the next town, who was selling pups for cheap. Bo'd named her Utah after seeing a picture in a travel book. 'It just seemed like a nice place,' she said.

But there were things I still didn't know about Bo Dickinson. Like why, after spending the night, she was always gone when I woke up in the morning. Or why she never invited me to her house.

But I got my answer to the second question a few days before Christmas.

It was winter break, and Gracie had gotten a ride home with some boys from UK. Even though she'd been home almost a week, I'd barely seen her. At night, she

172

went out with some of her friends from high school. During the day, she slept. But that Friday, Mama sent us shopping, giving us a long list of the things she'd need for Christmas dinner.

We made an extra stop at the Goodwill, though. Gracie said she wanted to look at the homecoming dresses people had donated because there was a spring dance coming up and she needed something to wear. While she dug through the layers of tulle and taffeta, I stayed near the front of the store, listening to the chime of the bells as people walked in and out in a hurry. A lot of people in Mursey did their Christmas shopping at the Goodwill, so this was a real busy time of year.

The donated books were up front, and I started going through a stack of them. I couldn't read the pages in most books, but if the letters were big and bright enough on the covers, I could at least make out their titles. And since about half the stack seemed to be made up of romance novels, some of those titles were pretty funny.

But one book, a heavy, leather-bound thing, got my attention. It was beat-up real bad. I could feel the scratches and creases of the cover. But the words in thick gold cursive still seemed to shine.

Our Poems: A Collection

'All right, let's go,' Gracie said, suddenly at my

shoulder. 'The only dresses in my size are maroon and yellow. So there's no chance in hell that's happening . . . What're you looking at?'

'Nothing,' I said. 'Just a gift for somebody.'

I bought the book for a couple dollars, then we got back into Gracie's car and started for home.

When I knew we were getting close to home, I said, 'Hey, Gracie, can you . . . can you drop me off at the church?'

'What for?'

'My friend lives in the trailer down the street. I wanna give her this.' I tapped the book in my lap.

The car slowed to a stop, and I heard the ticking of the turn signal. 'That's a Dickinson trailer, isn't it?'

'Yeah.'

'Some of my friends told me they'd heard you two were friends now,' Gracie said. 'I didn't believe them, though. Not until Mama said she'd been hanging out at the house.'

'Uh . . . well, yeah. It's true. So will you drop me off?'

Gracie sighed as the car turned right. 'Fine. But if Mama gets pissed—'

'She won't be mad.'

It was only half a lie. I hadn't asked permission to do this. Not from my parents. Not from Bo. I hadn't even known I was gonna have Gracie drop me off until five minutes ago. It was impulsive and spontaneous. And those were things I definitely wasn't allowed to be.

But Daddy was at work, and Mama was visiting my grandmother. As long as I was home before either of them, it'd be all right. And as much as my sister might have disapproved of me hanging out with Dickinsons, I knew she'd never get me in trouble with our parents.

That's how it had always been. Gracie and me might be different in every way – from how we looked to how we acted – but we were always a united front when it came to our parents. She'd definitely opposed them more than I had growing up, but now it was my turn to break the rules, and I knew she'd cover for me if it came down to that.

Gracie let me out in front of the church. But she couldn't stop herself from asking, 'Are you sure you can walk to her house on your own?'

I pretended I hadn't heard her and just started walking, my cane tapping its way down the sidewalk ahead of me.

Despite that, I did have a little trouble. I'd never actually stepped into Bo's yard before, just stood on the sidewalk in front of her trailer. So when I got there, it took a second for me and my cane to find our way across

175

the frozen yard and up the cement steps to her door. When I knocked, I heard Utah start barking inside.

'Hush!' I heard Bo yell. 'Ain't nobody trying to kill us, Utah. Jesus Christ.'

Then she opened the door. And froze.

'What're you doing here?' she asked after a second.

It wasn't the warm welcome I'd expected, and for a second, I was stunned. And scared. Like maybe she'd decided she didn't like me now. Maybe she realized what everyone else already knew – that I wasn't nearly the badass she thought I was.

'Um . . . I brought you something,' I said. 'Can I come in?'

'Well . . . Mama's not here, so yeah. Sure.'

I noticed the way she said it. Like, if her mother had been there, I wouldn't be welcomed in.

Bo stepped aside, and I walked into the trailer. First thing I noticed was how cold it was. Barely warmer than the December air outside. When I looked back at Bo, I noticed she looked wider than normal. Layers, I realized. No telling how many she had on.

The second thing that caught my attention was the soft sound of talking mixed with static coming from down the hall.

'What's that sound?' I asked.

176

'Police scanner,' Bo said. 'I keep it on all the time, just in case . . .' She trailed off. 'You said you brought me something?'

'Oh, yeah.' I reached into my coat pocket and pulled out the book from Goodwill. 'Thought you might like this. Merry Christmas.'

She took the book from my hands, but she didn't say anything. Not for a long second.

'Do you like it?' I asked.

Her voice cracked when she answered. 'I can't take this.'

'Why not?'

'Because I ain't got nothing for you,' she said. 'I wanted to get you something, but I just don't got the money to—'

'That's all right.'

'No. It's not.'

'Bo,' I said. 'It's a book from Goodwill. I didn't spend a lot. And . . .' I hesitated. 'Honestly? You know what I'd like in return? And it doesn't cost a thing?'

'What?'

'Can you read me some of those poems?' I asked. 'I'm still not real good with poetry. Still don't get it most of the time. But I love hearing you read it and explain it. That's all I want from you.'

177

Bo seemed to think on this for a second before saying, 'All right. I reckon I can do that.'

'Good.' I folded up my cane and tucked it under my arm as I looked around. The trailer was pretty dark, and the windows looked like they were covered with sheets instead of curtains.

Bo must've seen me looking, because she said, 'It ain't real nice, I know. Not like your house. But—'

'Can I see your room?' I asked.

She hadn't given me an answer yet when the front door burst open and Utah let out a startled bark from somewhere in the living room.

'Oh, shut up, you damn mutt,' a woman's voice snapped.

'Mama.' Bo sounded just as surprised as the dog. 'What're you doing here?'

'Live here, don't I?'

In the pale light, I could barely even make out her outline, though I still had a pretty good memory from the day when I'd first seen her in the front yard, screaming at the trees. 'Who's this?' she asked.

I guess she didn't remember that day quite as well.

'Uh . . . Mama, this is Agnes,' Bo said. 'Agnes Atwood.'

'Hi,' I said, giving a little wave in her general direction.

'Atwood,' Mrs Dickinson repeated. 'Your daddy

178

owns the hardware store, right?'

I nodded. 'Yes, ma'am.'

'I see a lot of people going in and out of there. Y'all must make a lot of money off that place.'

'Mama . . .'

'What? I'm just saying – it's great for her dad. Probably a pretty penny. Ain't it, Agnes? Y'all do pretty well for yourselves, I'd imagine.'

There was something strange about her voice. She sounded jumpy. Like she was teetering on the edge of something. And whatever it was, it made me nervous.

'You're friends with Bo now, huh?' she continued. 'She's always at your house these days. I hardly ever see her. You might as well be family. And since we're family, maybe you and your folks can help us out.'

'Mama, don't.'

'I'm only kidding!' Mrs Dickinson said. 'Agnes knows that. Right, Agnes?'

'Uh . . .' I glanced at Bo and wished I could make out her face in this light.

'But,' Mrs Dickinson continued, 'friends do help each other out, don't they? And we ain't had heat almost all winter. I'm just pointing out that they could help us, since y'all are so close now. A hundred bucks or so could go a long way. And that probably ain't nothing to y'all, Agnes. With the store doing well.'

I just stood there, not knowing what to do or say. Nobody had ever asked me for money before. Not even in this roundabout way. Where we lived, we grew up being taught never to ask for things like that. Never to put people on the spot. You waited until it was offered, and even then, you were supposed to say no at least once. I wasn't sure why. That was just the way it was. It was a rule everyone followed.

Everyone but Bo's mama, apparently.

'You oughta go to bed,' Bo told her. 'You seem tired.'

That's when it shifted. When the ledge Mrs Dickinson had been teetering on crumbled.

'Are you telling me what to do?' she yelled.

Bo, who'd moved to stand next to me, flinched. 'No. I'm just trying to help, Mama.'

'Bullshit! Don't you act like you're taking care of me. Why're you trying to get rid of me, huh? You embarrassed?'

'Mama—'

'Because I'm the one who oughta be embarrassed,' she hissed. 'You think I ain't heard? I know you been whoring around town, Bo. I ain't stupid. I'm the one who oughta be embarrassed of my slut of a daughter.'

Bo's hand closed around mine. 'Let's go, Agnes.'

'Wait a minute,' Mrs Dickinson said. 'Is that why she's here? You fucking her, too? Gone through all the men in town, so you gotta start sleeping with girls, too?'

'Come on,' Bo said to me. She tugged my hand and started leading me away, down a hallway I hadn't even noticed before.

'Don't you walk away from me!'

There was a loud thud and the sound of glass shattering behind me.

Close behind me.

Bo yanked me harder, and we started running toward the trailer's back door.

'You leave, you better not come back tonight! You hear me, you little dyke?' Mrs Dickinson hollered just as Bo threw open the back door and we tumbled out, down another set of cement stairs, with Utah at our heels.

Bo didn't even bother shutting the door behind us, so we could still hear her mother yelling as we ran, fast as we could, into the woods.

Our shoes slapped against the frozen ground and the December wind stung our faces as we bolted through the woods. We didn't stop until we reached the clearing, the place where Bo had come across me lost in the grass the day my parents drove Gracie to college. So much had changed for Bo and me since then that it felt like a lifetime had passed, not just a few months.

Bo let go of my hand and I slumped against a tree, panting to catch my breath. It was light out, but the sky was overcast and grey. Still, I could see Bo standing a few feet away, unmoving, arms wrapped around herself while Utah sniffed at the ground around us.

We were quiet for a long time, just standing there, shivering. I felt like I ought to say something, but I wasn't sure what. I had lots of questions, lots of concerns about Bo and her mom, but it felt wrong to ask. Still, the quiet was getting to me. So I said the first thing – the only thing – I could think of.

'Tell me something I don't know about you.'

She hesitated, and I wondered if maybe she'd get mad at me for trying to start our game at a time like this. But after a second she said, 'You first.'

'Um . . . Sometimes – not too often, but sometimes – I trip people with my cane on purpose, then act like it was an accident, like I didn't see them, so they can't get mad at me.'

She chuckled. Just a little. Short and quiet.

'I did it to Isaac Porter last week,' I went on.

Her laugh was a little louder this time.

'In church.'

She really cracked up then. It only lasted a second,

but her giggle filled me with relief. And I told myself it was gonna be OK. As long as I could make her laugh, make her smile, everything would be OK.

'You're going to hell,' she teased.

'What? No. Don't you know? Poor little blind girls never go to hell. We're all angels.'

'Oh, that's right. I must've forgot.' She walked over to the tree and leaned against the large trunk, her shoulder brushing my arm. 'Guess it's my turn now, huh?'

I nodded.

'I . . . have been in foster care before.'

I turned to look at her, surprised. 'Really? When?'

'Summer before eighth grade. Mama got arrested. Possession, I think. Don't really remember. But social workers came and got me in the middle of the night. I begged them to take me to my dad, but they said they didn't know where he was at. I ain't sure how hard they really looked, but . . . they took me to this house about an hour from here . . . I was only there a couple weeks, until she got out on bail, but . . . it was awful.'

I felt the dull ache of dread in my stomach, and I groped for her hand, squeezed it. It was bare and felt cold, even through my glove.

'There were a lotta kids there. Some, like me, were only there a few days. Some had been there for years.

183

There were a couple babies, too. They cried all the time. And the older kids were always fighting. I saw one of them pull a knife on the other. But the foster parents didn't do nothing about it. They wanted nothing to do with us. Well, except the dad. He was always walking in on the girls while we were changing or . . .'

She trailed off, and as awful as it sounds, I was glad. I didn't think I could hear any more. I already felt sick, just trying to imagine what living like that might be like. And, deep down, I felt guilty. Guilty because I'd always had a safe home, because I'd never had to worry about knives or creepy dads. And I'd never even thought to be grateful for that before.

'Living with Mama's no picnic, but I'm so scared, Agnes. That's why I'm always listening to that police scanner. I'm always waiting to hear her name. I'm so scared she's gonna get arrested again. If she does . . .'

When she didn't finish the sentence, I pushed. 'What?'

'I can't do it again,' she murmured. 'If she's arrested again, I'm taking off. I ain't gonna stick around and wait for CPS to come get me.'

'Oh . . .'

We were both quiet again, then Bo said, her voice shaking, 'You know . . . what she said . . . about me and you. Agnes, I don't – just because I like girls, too, don't mean I—'

'I know.'

'I just don't want you worrying that I—'

'I don't,' I assured her.

And it was true. I still wasn't sure how I felt about Bo's secret. We hadn't talked about it since that first night in my bedroom. But as uncertain as I felt, this was not something that had ever crossed my mind or made me uncomfortable. I knew her better than that.

'I just—'

'Bo, you don't have to explain to me. Ever.'

'Good.' She sighed. 'That's just another reason I can't tell nobody but you. Everyone around here already thinks I'm a slut. If they got wind I liked girls, too, they'd think I was going around trying to fuck everybody. Even my own mama thinks so.'

'Bo . . .'

'It's all right,' she said.

But it wasn't. It definitely wasn't all right.

Bo was always so strong, so tough, that hearing her voice shake like that, hearing the pain and the fear, just about killed me.

I wanted to hurt everyone who'd ever hurt her. I wanted to go back to that trailer and cause her mama the kind of pain her words had caused Bo. I wanted to hunt down and punish every goddamn gossip who'd ever spread the rumours about her, called her names, made her feel ashamed and alone. Even if that was just about everyone in Mursey.

Even if it included me.

The thought made my heart drop into my stomach. I'd only been friends with Bo for a few months, but the memory of standing with Christy on the steps of the church, being one of those town gossips myself, felt like a different lifetime. And now, the idea of her going anywhere, of her leaving me, was about the scariest thing I could imagine.

'Bo . . . would you really run away?' I asked after another long, quiet stretch.

'I don't want to,' she said. 'But . . . yeah. If I got to, I'll run.'

BO

There are sirens blaring by the time we get back to the car. I toss Utah into the back while Agnes dives into the front seat. It ain't a second later that our tyres are squealing and the car is speeding into the dark.

For a while, the only sound in the car is our heavy breathing. And as I drive, I can feel my eye starting to swell.

'Well,' Agnes says after ten minutes or so. 'What's next?'

'That wasn't enough for you?'

She laughs. 'That's not what I meant. But it's late and we can't just show up at your dad's house in the middle of the night. We ought to park somewhere and find some place to sleep.'

I almost argue, because we ain't gone very far today, but I don't. Not because showing up at Daddy's after midnight is such a bad idea – it don't really matter what time I show up – but because, even after what just happened, I ain't ready for all this to end just yet.

So I find a gravel road that seems real deserted. It weaves like a thread through a thick patch of woods. I follow it about a mile in, the car bouncing along, tossing us around a bit, before I pull off to the side. We park beneath a small patch of moonlight that's bleeding through the leaves.

I shut off the car and we lean our seats way back. Utah shifts in the backseat, trying to get comfortable.

'Bo?'

'Yeah?'

'Why'd you do it?'

'Do what?'

'Fight that guy.'

I turn my head to look at her. 'You heard what he called you.'

'Yeah, I know, but . . .' She pauses, then rolls to face me, too, even though I know she can't see nothing in this dark. 'People call you names all the time. And you don't do anything about it. I used to think it didn't hurt you at all, but now . . .'

I swallow. She ain't gotta finish the sentence.

. . . but now I know you're weak.

Maybe that's not how she'd say it, but it's the truth.

I might be loud and crude sometimes, but I bruise easy, and I don't heal real well. But I told her that a long time ago – that I was no Loretta Lynn.

'The only times I've ever seen you get into a fight – or get close – were when people said rude things about me or your mama. How come?'

'I dunno,' I say. 'Guess it's just easier to fight for people I love.'

'Do . . . do you love your mama?'

I'm surprised by her asking, and I think she is, too. Because she immediately starts talking again.

'Sorry. That's an awful thing to ask. Of course you do. I just—'

'I . . . love her when she's sober,' I say. 'Lately that's not real often, but . . . she's not always so bad.'

Every so often, Mama would stay clean for a week. Maybe two, if I was lucky. And things would start out good. She'd offer to take me and Colt to the movies in the next town, even though we barely had the money to pay for electricity. She'd start a new job at the grocery store or doing telemarketing, and she'd come home all happy and excited about it. She'd even cook and ask me to help, the way Daddy used to, and we'd sit on the sofa together, watching our old black-and-white TV with the bad reception.

And for a day or two . . . or three, we'd be a real mother and daughter.

I loved that side of Mama.

But when she was using, when she called me a slut or asked my best friend for money, she got a little harder to love.

'Well,' Agnes says, 'thank you. No one's ever really fought for me before. Except Mama, I guess.'

'Your mama's gotten into a fight?'

Agnes chuckles. 'Not like that. Not with fists or anything. You know . . . like if the school isn't helping me with the stuff I need or if some restaurant don't have a braille menu – that's when she fights.'

'Do you miss her?'

I hate myself for asking, because I ain't sure what I want the answer to be.

Agnes thinks for a while. 'Yeah. I do. This is the longest I've been away from her or Daddy. So it's just kind of strange, you know? To be away from them. Even if it is what I wanted – what I still want.'

I don't say anything to that.

For a minute, the only sounds are the cicadas and the soft hoot of an owl overhead.

'Hey,' Agnes says. 'You brought that book of poetry, right?'

'Yeah.'

'Can you read one?'

I almost laugh. 'It's not bright enough to read.'

'Really?' She sounds surprised. 'Wow. I guess sometimes I'm still confused by how much y'all sighted people can see. Maybe just as confused as y'all are about how much I see. So moonlight's not enough to read by?'

'Maybe if it's a full moon. And a clear night. But usually not.'

'I guess I learn something new every day.'

We both laugh, then Agnes yawns.

'Probably for the best. We ought to get some sleep.'

'Yeah. All right.'

'Good night, Bo.'

'Night.'

But while Agnes starts snoring within a couple minutes, it takes me a while to fall asleep. It ain't my first time sleeping in a car, but it never gets easier. Not because it's uncomfortable – I can handle that – but because it's too quiet.

I ain't gone a night sleeping without the TV turned on in years. I think I started keeping it on after Daddy left. The voices, even turned down low, just made me feel safer. Less alone.

But now there's no TV. Just Agnes's snoring and some

191

crickets chirping, and it ain't enough to help me sleep.

I think of turning on the car, playing the radio, but it'd kill the battery. So I just have to lie here, in the quiet, trying to ignore that familiar ache of loneliness and the guilty voices in my head.

AGNES

We had our first fight on New Year's Eve.

It was only a couple days before Colt would be moving out of Mursey and starting his new job, so Bo had suggested the three of us go to Tanner Oakley's party. The only trouble was, there was no way Mama would agree to me staying out until after midnight. Not at a party. Not anywhere.

I'd pretty much written off the idea until the Thursday night before, when Daddy had asked, 'So, honey. I know y'all have had your differences lately, but are you staying at Christy's for New Year's? It's sort of your tradition, right?'

'Uh, no, I . . .' But then it hit me. If my parents thought I was staying at Christy's, I'd be able to stay out all night without worrying about a curfew or anything. So I cleared my throat. 'I mean, yeah. We worked things out. I, uh . . . I think she's volunteering at the church that day, so if you could just drop me off there, I'll leave with her.'

'No problem,' Mama said. 'I'm glad you two worked it out.'

'Me too.'

Good old Christy – doing me more favours now than in the ten years we'd been best friends.

Bo and Colt picked me up at the church, then we headed over to Tanner's. The plan was for us to ring in the New Year there before heading back to Colt's place. We were gonna have popcorn and watch movies and stay up all night.

Unfortunately, things went downhill before we got to any of that.

It was close to midnight, and Colt and Bo had stayed sober. Colt was the designated driver, but Bo, I realized, never seemed to drink. Me, on the other hand, I'd had a couple already. And while I wasn't quite drunk, I think the combination of alcohol and me being sadder than I expected about Colt moving away was partly to blame for some of what got said that night.

'We could go in February. You can get a few days off, right, Colt?'

We were standing in Tanner's kitchen, leaned up

against the counter while George Jones's 'He Stopped Loving Her Today' played on a radio in the corner. Not exactly party music. I took another drink from my red cup, trying to hide the frustration I was feeling.

Bo hadn't given up on that road trip to Nashville she'd suggested months ago. I'd tried to tell her more than once since then that I didn't think it could happen, but I guess it wasn't sinking in, because she just kept at it. She made all sorts of plans about the places we'd see and the route we'd take and how good it would feel to get out of Mursey.

And I wanted all that. I wanted it so bad.

Which was the reason I was getting so annoyed. It was bad enough to be trapped here, but worse when Bo kept acting like there was some chance of escape.

I just wanted her to stop.

'Don't y'all have school?' Colt asked.

'Since when do you care about school?' Bo asked, laughing.

'Agnes might care.'

'Agnes wants to get out of town as much as I do.'

'Agnes can talk,' I said.

'Good,' Bo said. 'Then tell him why we gotta go to Nashville.'

'No.'

'What?' Bo sounded surprised, but I didn't know how she could be.

'I'm not going to Nashville with you, Bo.' It came out harsher than I'd meant it. Apparently, a couple beers made me a little mean.

'Why not?' she asked. 'This was our plan.'

'No. It's *your* plan,' I said. 'There's no way my parents will let me. You know how they are.'

'You ain't even asked them yet,' she pointed out, still sounding confident. 'It's just Nashville. It ain't that far.'

'Bo, I had to lie to even be here tonight,' I reminded her. 'They're never gonna let me go to Nashville for a week, during the school year. Not with you. Not with anybody. It's never gonna happen.'

'You ain't even asked them,' she repeated. And now she sounded like the one who was frustrated.

'All right,' Colt said, his voice tinged with a hint of nervous laughter. 'Maybe we should—'

'I don't gotta ask them. There's no point.'

'You're always talking about wanting to get out of Mursey.' She was getting mad now. Her voice raising just a little bit, but enough that I noticed. 'Well, here's your chance. Why're we arguing about it?'

I slammed my cup down on the counter, sloshing beer onto the sleeve of my sweater. 'Because not everyone can just take off for a week and leave the state, Bo. Not everyone can just decide when they wanna skip school in the morning and know no one's gonna punish them. Some of us actually have families that give a shit about us.'

I knew the second I said it that I shouldn't have.

I could blame it on the beer if I wanted. Or on my weird, secret crush on Colt making me crazy and clouding my judgment. But deep down, I knew it was mostly me. Me and my jealousy. Not of Bo's situation with her parents – I didn't want that – but of the freedom it gave her. Of the fact that she really thought she could just go to Nashville for a few days. No worries. No consequences. I didn't have that. Nothing close to that. And the more Bo talked about these plans, the more angry and jealous I got.

But now, I'd crossed the line.

For a minute, no one spoke. There was no sound but the radio and some drunk boys singing in the next room.

Then Bo pushed herself away from the counter. 'Happy fucking New Year,' she muttered.

'Where are you going?' Colt asked. When she didn't answer and just kept walking toward the door, he hollered at her. 'Bo! Where the hell are you going?'

'Getting a ride home!' she yelled back at us.

'Bo!'

But she didn't come back, and he didn't follow her. Instead, Colt turned to look at me.

I'd been having dreams about the two of us being alone for months, but this wasn't quite how I'd pictured it happening.

'Damn it,' I said, looking at my cup still sitting on the counter. Then, after a second, I dumped it into the sink. I wasn't gonna be having any more tonight.

In the next room, the boys started singing louder, belting out 'Family Tradition' a cappella, at the top of their lungs and way off-key. It didn't mix well with the heartache in George Jones's voice on the radio.

Colt sighed. 'Wanna get out of here?'

I looked at him. I couldn't see his face, but he didn't sound mad at me. He should've been, though, after what I'd just said. But instead, he just sounded tired.

There was a crash and some laughter from the room full of singing guys next to us.

'Yeah,' I said. 'I'm ready to go.'

BO

I wake up with Utah's tongue lapping at my cheek. I groan and look at her. She's got this big doggie grin on her face, like she's real proud of herself. Outside, the sun is up, light shining down through the tree. The bruised skin around my eye is throbbing a little.

'Finally,' Agnes says. Her seat's already propped back up. 'I was starting to worry you'd never wake up.'

I stretch and readjust my seat. 'Sorry.'

'It's all right. We both needed some rest.' She combs her fingers through her short, tangled hair and tries to fix the shirt that's sticking to her skin. 'But we better get moving, don't you think?'

She's right. There's a chance the police from that town are still looking for the two girls who got into the fight at the street fair last night. And my black eye would be an easy way to recognize us now. We're lucky

199

this road seems to be just as deserted and unused as I'd hoped.

I take Utah for a quick walk through the woods, letting her sniff around for a few minutes before she finally pees. Then she looks at me with big, expecting eyes, and I gotta look away. Because I ain't got a thing to feed her.

'Don't worry,' Agnes says, reading my mind as I climb back into the Reliant K. 'We'll be at your daddy's in a few hours. Once we get the money from him, we can stop by a pet store.'

We'll be at my daddy's in a few hours.

That nauseous feeling in my stomach, the one I've been fighting for days, gets worse all of a sudden. And it don't get any better as the ride goes on.

Agnes is feeling good. Smiling and laughing and talking about our future, even as I try to hold back the panic burps that keep rising in my throat.

'I had a real nice dream last night,' she says once we're a good hour into the day's drive. 'We'd found this little apartment and we had Utah and a cat, like we talked about yesterday. And you were working at a bookstore, and you kept bringing home books to read. And Colt came to visit. Doesn't that sound nice?'

'Yeah . . . sure does.'

200

'Anyway, it got me thinking,' she says, 'where do you think we ought to live? Once we get the money, I mean.'

'Um . . .' I focus on the turn, my hands tight on the steering wheel. 'I dunno.'

'The mountains seem nice. And a little one-bedroom might not be too expensive. And if we can get to your daddy's house today, we could start looking tomorrow, right?'

'Yeah . . . maybe.'

'We might have our own place this time tomorrow.' She laughs. A big, loud laugh that startles me a little. 'Sorry, I just . . . I never thought I'd get to live anywhere but Mursey. Hell, I never thought I'd get out of my parents' house. This might not be the way I wanted to go about doing it, but I'm just . . . I'm excited.'

In the rearview mirror, I can see that my face has gone green.

'We'll fill a bookshelf with nothing but poetry. Maybe we could even paint the walls. I've always liked the idea of painting my bedroom blue.'

'Agnes . . .'

'I know, I know. I'm getting ahead of myself. We don't have the money for all that yet. And it's probably gonna be real tough until we both turn eighteen, since we'll have to keep our heads down. But still. It's nice to think

201

about, you know? To have something nice to look forward to.'

I swallow hard and take a few deep breaths, trying to settle my stomach. The mountains are up ahead, round and misty and bluish grey. Like smoke drifting closer and closer.

'I know it's gonna be tough,' she goes on. 'I've never had to rough it before, and it's gonna be a challenge. But, honestly? It just . . . It feels so good to be free. To not have Mama and Daddy breathing down my neck, panicking over everything I do.' She reaches across the console and grabs my hand. 'But we're gonna be all right. Just you and me.'

I swerve into the parking lot of a gas station so fast that the tyres squeal. Utah slides across the backseat with a yelp, and Agnes gasps. I slam my foot on the brakes, barely missing another car. We ain't even in a real parking spot when we come to a stop.

I barely hear Agnes say, 'What are we doing?' before I shove open the car door, lean out, and throw up on the pavement.

'Oh my God! Bo?'

I sit up and wipe my mouth with the back of my hand.

'Did you just throw up?' Agnes asks.

'Yeah.'

'Are you OK?'

'Fine.' I lean back in the seat, closing my eyes for just a second. 'Must've just ate something bad.'

'The barbecue last night? We ate the same things. And I feel all right.'

'I dunno, then. But I'm fine.' I shut the door and shift gears, backing the car up so we're in line with the gas pump.

'What are we doing?' she asks.

'We're almost out of gas. And we should probably grab something to eat.'

'Do we have the money?'

'I got a little left.'

We both climb out of the car, and I roll down a window for Utah. Agnes leans against the side of the Reliant while I pump, still talking about the apartment we'll get once we find Daddy. I don't hear much of what she says, but I nod along anyway.

I don't fill the tank. We ain't got the funds for that. But I give us just enough to hopefully get the beat-up car the rest of the way. I put the nozzle back and start walking toward the little convenience store. Agnes walks next to me, her cane dragging across the pavement.

'We ought to get something for the dog, too,' Agnes

says once we're inside.

There's a loud air conditioner blasting and the man behind the counter's got the local news on a tiny black-and-white TV. The store's real small. There ain't much in the way of people food, never mind dog food.

'Guess we could get something to share with her.'

'Like what?'

'Bologna? That's what I've fed her before when Mama's forgotten to pick up the dog food.'

Agnes wrinkles her nose. 'Ugh. I hate bologna.'

'Well, I can't think of anything besides lunch meat. You got something else in mind?'

'I'm guessing a lobster dinner is out of the question, huh?'

I force a laugh, and Agnes smiles.

'I'm OK with lunch meat. We can make sandwiches.'

'Just not bologna sandwiches.'

'Definitely not.'

I grab some ham and cheese. Utah will be happy with both. Then I grab a loaf of bread, and we walk to the counter. The cashier, an old man with a big white beard, looks up from the TV.

'Afternoon,' he says, picking up the package of ham. 'How're y'all today?'

'Not too bad, thanks,' I say, putting our food on the counter.

He looks surprised and stares at me for a second. Probably thought I was a boy until I started talking. But then he stares harder, and when his eyes shift to Agnes, I think I might throw up again.

'Wait a second . . .' he says.

Fuck. I start backing away, real slow at first. There's a chance he might not recognize me with the big shiner on my eye and the short hair, but Agnes . . .

'I know you,' he says, looking at her. 'I've seen your face.'

'Uh . . . I don't think so,' Agnes says, but if I can hear her voice shaking, I know he can, too.

Shit, shit, shit. I reach for her hand.

'Nah, I have . . .'

My fingers close around hers.

'Wait! Y'all are the girls from the news.'

'Run!'

I nearly pull Agnes's arm out of its socket when I bolt for the door. She keeps up, though, and we burst out of the store at a sprint. I only let go of her hand when we reach the car. Inside, Utah's barking, panicked. I yank open the driver's-side door and climb in. It takes Agnes a second as she fumbles for the handle.

'Come on!' I yell.

She pulls the door open and throws herself inside. She ain't even closed it all the way when I take off.

The tyres screech and I smell burnt rubber as I speed out of the parking lot. In the rearview, I can see the cashier, standing in front of the store, shouting words I can't hear and waving what looks like a loaf of bread in his hand.

'We didn't pay for the gas,' Agnes says.

'That's what you're thinking about right now?' I make a sharp turn and see Agnes grip the door for dear life. 'We got bigger problems than stealing a few dollars of gas.'

'Sorry, but I've never stole anything before.'

'Except your sister's car.'

'It's not the same.'

I yank the wheel too hard, and the Reliant K skids, almost missing the turn onto a gravel back road.

'Where are we going?' Agnes asks. She sounds scared. I'm scared, too.

Running from the street fair last night was different. No one had recognized us. As long as the cops didn't get a look at our faces, we were gonna be OK. But now, if that cashier calls 911, the police will be out looking for us, for our car. Not just two random teenagers.

'We're getting off the main road,' I say. 'So no one'll see us.'

'But we'll get lost.'

'We'll be fine.'

She's right, though. It ain't twenty minutes before we're weaving our way down into a holler with the shadowy mountains rising up around us. And I've got no clue where we're at.

'We've got to ask for directions, Bo,' Agnes says.

'No! They'll recognize us like the guy at the store. They'll call the cops. This car's licence plate might already be on the news.'

'It's better than getting lost out here!' she argues.

'No, it's not. And I'll find the way. Just give me a damn minute!'

It's the first time I've ever yelled at her, and it makes me feel more like a monster than any of the other awful things I've done.

But there's no one to ask for help anyway. What Agnes can't see is that there's not a whole lot around us. We passed a few trailers a mile or two back, but now, there's nothing. Just the big, smoky hills and this narrow little road.

There's no street signs, neither, which ain't helping me at all.

I press my foot on the gas again, speeding up and looking for something – anything – that might tell me where the hell we are.

'Slow down!' Agnes yells as I swerve to avoid some roadkill.

'Just let me think!' I yell back.

In the backseat, I hear Utah whine.

The gravel turns to dirt, and the path takes a tight turn. I throw my weight into the steering wheel. The car tilts, and for a second, I'm sure we're about to flip over, to roll down the hill in a pile of metal and breaking glass. For just a second, I think Agnes and I are gonna die out here.

But somehow I manage to right the car, and we're back on the road. Only now, Agnes looks petrified and Utah is barking and my heart is pounding so hard it feels like someone is firing a shotgun inside my chest.

'We're gonna be all right,' I say. I mean to sound comforting, but I don't think I do.

And right then, I hear it. Agnes does, too.

A loud pop!

'Goddamn it! Motherfucker!' I scream, slamming my fist into the steering wheel.

The car slows to a stop.

'What just happened?' Agnes asks.

I bury my face in my hands. My whole body is shaking, and I ain't sure she can hear me when I answer.

'Motherfucking flat tyre.'

AGNES

'I crossed the line, didn't I?'

The beer buzz was long gone.

We were back at Colt's mama's trailer. She was out for the night, and it was just Colt and me there. Alone.

I always thought it would be exciting or maybe a little scary to be alone with a boy – especially one I liked – but right now, all I was feeling was guilt and regret.

Colt didn't answer my question, which I knew meant yes, I had. I'd done more than crossed the line. I'd trampled on it.

'I can't believe I said that.' I sat down on the edge of his little twin bed.

His bedroom was tiny. Smallest bedroom I'd ever seen. But something about that made me feel safe. There were posters up on the walls, but I couldn't see what they were of. Sports teams, I figured. That's what all boys put on their bedroom walls. Other than that, though, the room seemed awful bare. And there were cardboard boxes packed and lined up all along the wall.

'It definitely wasn't the nicest thing I've heard you say,' Colt agreed, sitting down beside me.

'But she just kept pushing,' I told him. 'I know it doesn't justify it. But she just wouldn't listen. My parents aren't like hers. They barely let me breathe without being watched – let alone go to another state for a week without them.'

'Have you talked to them about that?' Colt asked. 'About how they treat you?'

'No. There's no point.'

'You don't know that.'

I groaned. 'Not you, too.'

'I ain't talking about Nashville. Forget about that,' he said. 'I'm just talking about you. You should tell them how you feel. They might listen. Might not start letting you run wild or nothing, but they might let you make a few choices, at least. Make it so you don't have to lie about where you're going.'

'Yeah . . . maybe.'

But I didn't believe it. I'd never realized just how tight my parents kept the leash until I met Bo. Maybe because, before that, I'd never been given a chance to pull at it.

Then she came along, and I had a reason to go out, to leave the house, to be like any other girl. And they didn't even want me walking home from the damn bus stop.

'Far as Bo goes . . .' He shook his head. 'Sometimes she wants things so badly, I think it hurts her. Blinds her.' He paused. 'Sorry. I shouldn't have—'

'It's fine,' I said.

'Anyway . . . She gets these ideas in her head. Ideas about going to Nashville, yeah, but ideas about people, too. And she holds on so tight she can't see when it's better to let go. Not until she gets let down. Sad part is, I think she expects people to let her down. But it ain't stopped her from wanting.'

'That's why she's Patsy,' I murmured.

'Huh?'

'Nothing . . . But maybe it's not sad. Maybe it's great she hasn't given up on wanting things.'

'Wanting things is dangerous when you're like us,' Colt said. Then he turned to look at me. And we were so close all of a sudden. I could see the colour of his eyes. That rich sweet-tea shade. 'It's different for you, though. I think you could stand to want for more.'

'I want things,' I said. I was thinking of something I wanted right then. Something I'd never wanted before he sat this close to me.

212

'Maybe, but you don't seem to do nothing about it. Bo chases what she wants, even if it ain't good for her. You act like you've done give up.'

I should've been mad about that. Should've told him that he barely knew me. How could he have a clue what I wanted or how much I wanted it? But it was hard to be mad when I knew he was right. I said I wanted out of Mursey, said I wanted my parents to treat me differently, but I never tried. Never pushed. Not like Bo.

I wasn't ready to fight for those other things. Not yet. But I could go after the thing I wanted now.

'I know you like Bo, Agnes. But be careful. It ain't easy to love a Dickinson.'

That didn't stop me, though. I leaned toward him and, before I could think twice, kissed Colt Dickinson.

It was quick. Fast. And I missed his mouth – hit right on the corner of his lips. I pulled back a little, wishing my eyes were good enough to really make out facial expressions.

Colt was quiet, and for a second I was scared I'd done something wrong. But then he leaned in, put his hands on my cheeks, and guided my mouth back to his.

I'd never been kissed before, and at first, I was worried I was doing it wrong. I wasn't sure about where to put my hands or how to tilt my head or what in God's name

I was supposed to do with my tongue.

But Colt seemed to know. He kept kissing me, and eventually, I picked up the rhythm and followed his lead. It was like that night we danced. It was fun and a little overwhelming and sometimes he'd take me by surprise. But that's what made it exciting.

It was also exciting to be the one doing the surprising. When I slid my hands down and found the hem of Colt's T-shirt, I tugged it up, wanting to pull it over his head. Colt hesitated, then laughed and sat back, letting me take it off him. He was scrawny, but when he wrapped his arms around me again, I could feel the subtle muscles in his arms and chest.

I'm not sure how we ended up lying down, twisted together on top of his bed. Or how my shirt and bra ended up on the floor. All I knew was, when Colt pulled back, broke our kiss, I felt cold and heartbroken.

But just then he was looking at me. At more of me than anyone else had seen. And I felt self-conscious. Colt Dickinson had probably seen way prettier girls naked. Skinnier girls. Tanner girls. I was round and pasty and not the kind of girl boys wanted to see shirtless.

Only, Colt didn't seem disgusted or amused at all. He ran a hand through my long hair, his fingers grazing my neck and shoulder. His hand slid down my arm, then to my stomach, my hip. And even though he didn't say a word, I realized that maybe Colt didn't see me the way I saw me. I gave him a nervous smile before he leaned back down to kiss me again.

The longer we kissed, the more aware I was that we should stop, and the less I wanted to.

I'd never been totally sure about waiting for marriage, but Colt wasn't even my boyfriend. He was leaving in a couple days, and who knew when or if I'd see him again. It was gonna be hard enough saying goodbye when all I had was a crush, but now . . .

He pulled away again, breathing hard. 'Agnes . . .'

I didn't let him finish. I grabbed for him, yanked him back down to me. Because every second we weren't touching felt like agony.

He laughed. 'OK . . . But . . . You sure this isn't too fast?'

'I'm sure. I want this.'

Truth be told, it probably was too fast. All the firsts weren't supposed to come at once. But I'd spent my whole life standing still. And I didn't want to be still anymore. Because as much as I knew doing this and then letting Colt leave would hurt, I was sure the regret of doing nothing would be worse.

Sleeping with a boy who wasn't my boyfriend, who'd

be gone by the end of the week – it sure hadn't been part of my plan. But, then again, neither had becoming friends with Bo. And regardless of our fight tonight, I didn't regret that for a minute.

So I decided to do what Colt had said – I was going after what I wanted for once.

And, tonight, I was all right with moving too fast.

BO

'Of course this piece of trash ain't got a spare. Damn it.'
I slam my fist into the side of the car. My knuckles ache
a little, but I don't give a shit. The little dent I left in the
door is worth it.

'So . . . what now?'

Agnes is standing on the side of the road – if you can
even call it that. Our bags are by her feet, and she's
holding Utah's leash. The dog's just sniffing around. She
ain't got a clue anything's wrong.

I reach into the car and pull out the book of maps
Colt gave us. I open up the map of Kentucky, the one I
drew our route on, hoping I might be able to figure out
where we're at. I run my finger along the line, tracing our
trip, guessing where the gas station was. But I made so
many fast turns after that, trying to get out of town, that
I ain't even sure what direction we'd gone.

I keep looking, keep trying, but the tiny lines all start blurring together.

'Fuck,' I say, throwing the book to the ground and giving it a good stomp with my right foot. And another.

'Bo?' Agnes's voice is trembling.

I freeze, shame creeping up into my chest. Yelling, punching cars, tearing up books – my Dickinson is showing, and it ain't pretty. I take a deep breath and step away from the trampled maps. Then I run my hands through my hair. I keep forgetting how short it is now, and when I remember, it makes me wanna cry.

'Bo?' she says again.

'This road ain't on the map,' I say. 'I got no clue where we are or where to go.'

'Oh . . . So . . . What do we do?'

'Only thing we can do.' I take a deep breath and swallow back the tears before turning toward her. 'We gotta walk.'

'Walk where?'

I pick up our bags and sling them over my shoulder. It's lucky we don't got much. The bags are real light, which makes hauling them around a hell of a lot easier. 'We just keep following the path. It'll lead to a town eventually.'

'Yeah, but . . . how long is eventually?'

218

'You got a better idea?' I snap.

Agnes's eyes go wide, and I hate myself for being short with her. But the truth is, I ain't sure how long we'll have to walk. And we're deep enough in the mountains that the sun'll disappear come midafternoon. If we're too far out, it could take several hours to get back on a main road. And there ain't no lights out here. She can't see, and the ground's uneven with several steep slopes and ditches. Not sure how much help me or that cane is gonna be then.

'Fine,' Agnes says. She's gone a little cold, and it makes me feel even worse. 'Let's get going, then.'

She starts walking without me, and I hurry to catch up with her. 'Here,' I say, taking Utah's leash from her left hand. 'I'll take the dog. Hold on to my arm, all right? The ground is pretty rough around here.'

She takes my elbow, and we start walking. We don't say nothing for a long, long time. And I know I oughta apologize. For yelling at her. For getting us lost. For bringing her along to begin with. I oughta tell her I'm sorry.

I oughta tell her a lot of things.

Instead, though, neither of us talks for almost an hour. I reckon we're both too overwhelmed to say much.

Agnes is the first to break the silence, though.

'It's gonna be OK,' she says.

We're still walking, still on a dirt road where nobody seems to live. We've passed a couple trailers in the few miles we've gone, but they looked old and abandoned, grass grown up nearly as high as the broken windows.

My feet ache – these flip-flops ain't meant for hiking through mountains – and my stomach's started growling.

'How you figure?' I ask.

'You were right before,' Agnes says. 'We'll hit a town eventually. Maybe we can get a motel room. Just because the guy at the gas station recognized us doesn't mean everybody will. Could've just been a fluke.'

'Then what?' I ask. I don't even bother pointing out that that guy probably called the cops, who are probably out looking for us now. 'We ain't got a car. And I don't got a clue how to lead anybody back to the Reliant, even if we did find a spare tyre we could afford.'

'Well . . . Then maybe wherever we end up is the city we're meant to stay in,' she says. 'We can find a place and—'

'We can't.'

'Yes, we can. It'll be tough, but maybe we don't need your daddy's money,' she insists. 'You can get a job at a store or something. I can . . . I'm not sure what I can do, but I'll find something. We'll figure it out.'

My stomach starts aching again, and it ain't got nothing to do with hunger. 'Agnes . . .'

'If we really have to, we can call your daddy. Maybe he'll come to us.'

'Agnes—'

'Even if the place is real bad, it's all right. We'll save up. Then we can find a better place. With a yard and—'

'It ain't gonna happen, Agnes!' It comes out a scream, echoes through the holler. 'We ain't getting an apartment or jobs or a yard. It ain't gonna happen! It was never gonna happen!'

She drops my arm, backs up like I've burned her. 'What are you talking about?'

'I ain't looking for my daddy so we can get money, Agnes! I'm looking for him so I can live with him.'

Agnes stares at me, her mouth open just a little. The truth gets shouted back at us from a dozen directions. All the phantom voices have faded, though, before she says a word. Just one word.

'What?'

I'm shaking all over. My hands. My legs. And I think I might throw up again. Utah can tell something's wrong, too. She rubs her face against my leg, trying to comfort me. But it's no good.

I never meant to tell Agnes this way. Never meant to

221

scream it at her on a dirt road in the middle of nowhere. But now the words are out, and I can't bring them back.

'I wanna live with him.' I say it quiet enough so the eavesdropping mountains can't repeat the words. 'That's why I wanna find him. Not for money, but because I wanna see if he'll let me move in.'

'You . . . But I thought . . . You said—'

'I know,' I say. 'I lied, Agnes. I . . . I'm sorry.'

Everything goes still. Everything but my trembling hands and feet, at least. No birds fly over. Utah don't move, don't even sniff at the ground. Even the crickets have gone quiet, just for a second.

Then, slowly, Agnes turns. She holds her cane out in front of her, sweeping it along the dirt road as she starts moving in the direction we been headed for the past hour.

'Agnes?'

'It'll be dark in a few hours.' Her voice is like a bucket of ice water being dumped over my head. 'We better keep walking.'

AGNES

Colt drove me to Bo's house the next morning, and it was probably the most awkward five-minute drive of my whole life.

Last night, we'd fallen asleep, squeezed in his tiny bed, and it felt safe and easy. But something about daylight had shifted things. We hadn't said much to each other since we woke up, and I could barely look at him without feeling embarrassed.

Not that I regretted what had happened – I didn't. At all.

Just thinking about the night before gave me butterflies. Colt had been so patient and sweet and slow. And even when it was weird or uncomfortable, we'd mostly laughed through it. It was fun, and we'd been safe; Colt had used a condom. I had nothing to regret, honestly.

But still. When morning comes, what do you say to

223

the boy you shared your first kiss with, then slept with an hour later? Especially when that boy is leaving town the next day? I had no idea.

And Colt wasn't making things easier. I couldn't see faces real well, but I'd gotten pretty good at reading the energy in the room. And Colt's energy was uncomfortable. I might not have regretted last night, but maybe he did. Maybe he was wishing he hadn't slept with some stupid high school girl. Did he think I wanted him to be my boyfriend now?

Did I want him to be my boyfriend now?

The truck came to a stop as we pulled up in front of Bo's trailer. We both just sat there for a minute, the engine idling.

'So . . .' Colt said.

'So . . . You're leaving tomorrow, right?'

'Yeah. I'm . . . sorry.'

'For what? Leaving?'

'I guess.'

I let out a breath.

'Or, I dunno,' Colt said.

'You don't have anything to be sorry for.'

Another long pause.

I swallowed. 'So, I guess this is goodbye, then.'

'Yeah. Reckon it is.'

I finally got the nerve to look at him, and he was looking right back at me. And I started wondering how I was supposed to get out of this truck. Was I supposed to kiss him goodbye? Or just wave? Waving seemed kinda weird. But maybe kissing him did, too.

After neither of us moved for a second, I cleared my throat. 'Um, I should . . .'

'Yeah. All right.'

I reached for the handle and opened the door. But before I'd unfolded my cane, Colt said, 'Agnes?' And I turned back again.

He leaned forward and kissed me. On the cheek, not the mouth. Which was even more confusing, really. 'I hope y'all work it out,' he said.

'Thanks. Me too.' I slid out of the truck and looked back up one last time before shutting the door. 'See you, Colt.'

I stood in the yard and watched the truck drive away. Then I took a deep breath and tried to get myself together. I was here to see Bo. I should be thinking about her, not what I'd done with her cousin.

I tugged my coat a little tighter and turned around, heading for the front door. Just like last time, Utah started barking the minute I knocked. And a second later, the front door swung open.

'Agnes? What're you doing here?' She didn't sound angry, just surprised. Like she didn't think I'd show up. Like she didn't expect me to come and apologize.

'Colt dropped me off,' I told her. And I hoped saying his name didn't make me blush. 'I'm sorry. I know it's early. I just . . . Bo, I shouldn't have said that last night. The truth is, everything you were saying – all those adventures you had planned – those all sound great. Better than great. And I want to go on all of them with you. But I knew there was no way, so I got mad. And I'm real sorry.'

Bo sighed. 'Well, it ain't like anything you said was a lie.'

'I'm still sorry.'

'Yeah . . . Me too,' she said. 'I shouldn't have kept pushing.'

'You know if I could go, I would.'

'Yeah . . . Guess I just don't know what it's like to have parents like yours.'

'Ones that smother you half to death?'

'Ones that care.'

'Care too much.' There was a long pause where Bo didn't reply, so finally I asked, 'Do you wanna come back to my house? It's freezing out here, and Mama always makes a big dinner on New Year's Day.'

'Uh, sure. I guess. But don't your folks think you're with Christy?'

'I called and asked Gracie to pick me up at the church. My folks think Christy's volunteering there again today. I'll just tell them you walked by and I invited you over.'

Bo laughed. 'You're getting awful good at the lying.'

She said it like it was a compliment, but I wasn't so sure if lying was something I wanted to get good at.

Utah followed us to the church. There was snow on the ground, the sidewalks hadn't been shovelled just yet, and it crunched beneath my boots. Next to me, I could hear Bo's teeth chattering, and I wondered how many years she'd gone without a real winter coat or boots. But I didn't think that was the sort of thing I ought to be asking right then, so instead, we both stayed quiet.

We were standing on the front steps, waiting for my sister, when Bo said, so quiet I almost didn't hear, 'Thank you for coming today.'

'Of course. Did you think I'd just say something like that and never come apologize?'

She didn't answer, and I realized that's exactly what she thought. That we'd fight and never talk again. That I'd leave her, like so many others had before me.

'You're the most important person in my life,

Bo Dickinson,' I said. 'I don't know if I could make it without you. So no matter what we fight about, I'll still be around.'

She leaned her head on my shoulder just as a fresh flurry of snowflakes began to fall. 'I got a better idea,' she said. 'Let's promise to never fight again.'

'All right. I think I like that plan. So last night was the first and the last fight you and me will ever have.'

'Promise?' she asked.

'I promise.'

BO

Agnes ain't talking to me.

We've been walking for hours, and it's dark now. Real dark. There ain't no streetlights on this dirt road, and the mountains block out about half the stars. Even I can hardly see, but she still won't hold on to my arm. Insists she's better off just using the cane.

And maybe she is, I think, stumbling over a rough patch of ground.

The silence and the darkness and the hunger are starting to drive me crazy, though. And every time Utah, who's gotta be starving, whines up at me, I feel like the guilt might eat me alive. I can't control the dark or the food, but maybe I can get Agnes to talk to me if I try hard enough.

'Seems like I might need one of them canes,' I say.

She stays quiet.

Utah pulls on her leash, lunging after something I can't see. Maybe a rabbit or maybe just a cricket. She likes to chase both. But I pull her back. 'This damn dog,' I say to Agnes. 'Walking this long, and she ain't tired at all. Still trying to chase anything she sees.'

Nothing.

I don't think I've ever been cold-shouldered before. When Dickinsons are mad, you can't get us to stop yelling. But I think the quiet is worse.

A few minutes later, I give it another shot.

'Tell me something I don't know about you,' I say, hoping maybe our old game will get her talking to me.

But all she does is sigh.

'All right . . . I guess I'll go first,' I say. 'So, when we were kids, Colt nearly drowned me. We'd gone down to the river by ourselves to swim. He was twelve and I was ten. And he dared me to jump off that big wall – you know, the one by the Thomases' bait shop?'

She don't answer. Don't even look at me. Just keeps walking.

'Well, he dared me to jump. He went first, and he was fine. So I did. And I went under the water, but when I tried to come back up, I had a hard time. Colt hadn't thought about the current. I was so little, it about washed me downstream. Thank God he caught hold of me and pulled me up on a rock.'

I don't tell her the part about how I cried. Or how I was so mad at Colt for daring me to jump that I threw a rock at his head once we got back on dry ground. How I'm the reason he's got a scar right above his ear. I ain't even sure if Agnes knows about the scar. Her eyes probably ain't good enough to notice it.

And right about now, with how Agnes just keeps ignoring me, I'm wishing Colt hadn't bothered saving me at all. Maybe we'd both be better off if I'd just washed away that day.

I clear my throat and say, 'Your turn,' just as we round a curve and—

Light.

Headlights. Small, twin pinpoints of white way off in the distance, speeding past. They're far, but they're there.

I almost shout. Because that's a road – a real road – up ahead of us. And in a few more steps, I even spot what looks like the giant sign of a Shell gas station. We're probably still a quarter mile away, but that ain't nothing compared to how far we've already walked.

'Holy shit!' I shout. 'Agnes – can you see that? There are cars up there. And a gas station. Oh, thank God. Finally.'

Her voice is flat when she says, 'Good.'

'Good? It's great. If there are cars, then there are people and we can get a ride or—'

'Bo.'

'What?'

Agnes takes a deep breath, and then she plays the game I started. It's her turn, after all. And with the lights looming in the distance, she takes away all the relief and joy I just felt. She tells me something I didn't know.

Something I should've known was coming.

'I'm leaving, Bo,' she says. 'I'm going home.'

AGNES

I hadn't spoken to Christy in months. We sat on opposite sides of the room during Sunday school and kept our distance in English class. We crossed paths in the hallway at school a few times – and she bumped into me while I was at my locker once – but after a quick, mumbled sorry, she was gone.

But one day in mid-January, in the bathroom after lunch, the silence was unexpectedly broken.

I'd just turned on the tap to wash my hands when the door opened. I didn't bother looking to see who'd just come in. The bathrooms weren't lit real well, and in the weak yellow light, even people's hair, the easiest feature for me to see, didn't look very distinct. But the minute I heard her voice, I knew it was Christy.

'I covered for you on New Year's.'

I was so surprised that I jumped, splashing a little

water on my shirt. And then Christy was next to me, checking her hair in the mirror.

'Your mama called. Said she figured you wouldn't have reception so it was easier to call my house. Luckily, it was just me and Andrew, so I told her you were in the bathroom. She was very happy you and I worked things out.'

I couldn't quite figure out the tone in her voice. She didn't sound mean or threatening, or even passive-aggressive. She didn't sound like anything, really.

'Oh. Um . . .' I pumped the soap into my hands. 'Sorry about that. And . . . thank you.'

'No problem.' She was quieter than I remembered. 'So . . . Andrew and I are officially engaged. He gave me the ring on Christmas.' She holds up her hand, and I smile, even though I could never see something as small as an engagement ring.

'That's great, Christy. Congratulations.'

'Thanks . . . I almost called you. When he did it. For some reason I really wanted to tell you, but . . .' She trailed off, cleared her throat, then turned on her own tap. 'Anyway. We're not gonna get married for a while. Maybe summer after next.'

It was so surreal, after our fight back in the fall, to be standing with Christy, having a quiet, friendly conversation. After a month or two of her ignoring me, I'd eventually realized Christy and me weren't friends anymore. It sounds silly, but I guess I'd assumed we'd eventually work it out. Not that we'd ever be the way we had been before, but . . . I hadn't realized it was over until it had been over for a while.

I never really thought we'd talk again after all this time. And certainly didn't think she would be showing me her ring and covering for me when Mama called to check in.

Which was a whole other problem. I'd honestly thought I was safe on New Year's Eve. That telling a simple lie would be enough. Clearly, I was underestimating how close an eye my parents wanted to keep on me. I didn't even think that was possible.

I rinsed my hands and turned off the water. I was halfway to the paper towel dispenser when I couldn't hold it in anymore and had to spin around and ask, 'Why did you lie for me?'

Christy sighed and shut off her own tap. 'I don't know,' she said. 'I guess I just . . . Your parents have always been so overprotective. It used to drive me crazy. And it drove me crazy even more because you wouldn't do anything about it. I guess I was kinda proud of you for breaking the rules.'

I almost pointed out the irony of that. The big fight we had was about sin, and here she was saying she was proud of me for disobeying my parents. But we'd done so well being friendly, and I didn't wanna fight with her again. So I just nodded and said, 'Well, thank you.'

'But . . .' She hesitated. 'Look, I know I'm the last person you probably care to listen to right now. It's just . . . I'm glad you're fighting their rules because they're ridiculous sometimes, but lying to them won't change a thing.'

'Christy . . .'

'I'm not always gonna be there to answer the phone when they call,' she said. 'You gotta talk to them, Agnes.'

I groaned. 'Yeah. Bo says the same thing.'

'Wow. Never thought I'd agree with Bo Dickinson on anything.' And I heard that touch of meanness in her voice again, that old Christy was all too familiar. But then she let out a breath and said, 'You just got to stand up to them, Agnes. The way you stood up to me.'

I didn't have a clue what to say to that. I didn't know if I was supposed to say anything. Luckily, the bell rang and gave me an excuse to keep quiet.

I dried my hands and tossed the paper towel in the trash. 'Bye,' I said over my shoulder as I moved toward the door.

'Bye,' she replied. And then, just as the door was shutting, I heard her say one last thing. It wasn't an apology for the things she'd said about Bo. Or for the way she'd treated me like a burden. I doubted I'd ever get that from her. But I did get something. Three quiet words I almost didn't hear.

'I miss you.'

And, for me, that was enough.

It was February before I saw or heard from Colt again.

My parents had driven Bo and me to Marty's on a Saturday, even though I'd assured them we could walk. It was only a quarter mile down the road from our house, after all. And Daddy was always talking about how expensive gas was. But Mama insisted, saying the sidewalks were too slick – even though they'd all been shovelled well since the last snow a few days ago – and that she'd just 'feel better' if someone drove us.

Which also meant she'd be picking us up in an hour.

As Bo and I sat down in a booth with our fries and Cokes, Christy's words from a month earlier were whirling around in my brain. Had my parents really always been this overprotective? Had I just not noticed or cared much until Bo came along?

I was thinking so hard about this that I didn't even

notice the sound of a truck pulling up outside or the bells jingling over the front door. Bo must've, though, because she hollered Colt's name real loud and jumped out of the booth, running across the tiny restaurant to him.

'Thought I might find y'all here,' he said, giving her a hug.

Then the two of them headed back to the booth where I was sitting, frozen in midmotion as I reached for a fry.

I hadn't really thought about what it might be like seeing him again after what had happened on New Year's. Somehow, I guess I'd just assumed I wouldn't. Which, thinking about it now, was silly. He lived only a couple hours away, and of course he'd come back to see his mama and Bo sometimes. Still, I wasn't quite prepared.

Also, I hadn't told Bo about us sleeping together. I'd wanted to. Almost did on a few occasions. But every time I started to open my mouth, I chickened out. I didn't want Bo thinking I was some dramatic, needy girl who made a big deal about having sex. Not when she had so much experience and seemed to act like it was no big deal. I worried that if I told her about Colt, I'd also start telling her about how confused I felt. About how I'd always planned to lose my virginity to somebody I might have a future with. But, at the same time, I was happy I'd done it with Colt. And I did like him, but he was so far away and I had no idea what he thought of me and . . .

She'd probably think I was crazy. Or immature.

So I hadn't told her.

Which meant she had no idea why I was suddenly so quiet when they sat down.

'You all right, Agnes?' Bo asked. 'Something wrong with the fries?'

'No,' I said. 'I'm fine.'

Bo stared at me for a second, like she wasn't sure if she ought to believe me, but then she turned to Colt. 'So what're you doing here?'

'Visiting Mama for the weekend. And came to pick up the last of my stuff.'

'How's work?'

'It's all right. I get a lotta shit, since I'm the new guy. And the youngest. But it's money.'

They talked like this for a while, Bo drilling him with questions about his new apartment and what it was like living outside of Mursey. And I just sat there, hoping I didn't look as awkward as I felt. And, for the first time, wishing Mama's overbearing side would kick in and convince her to come pick us up early.

Not that I wasn't happy to see Colt again – I was.

239

I just had no clue what to say to him.

I was gonna have to come up with something, though, because a few minutes later the bell over the door jingled and a woman went up to the counter to order. None of us paid attention at first, but we all heard the gossip she told the cashier.

'That Dickinson woman is outside her trailer without a coat,' she was saying in a voice that sounded a lot like an elderly Christy might. 'Looks like she's trying to fix that lawn mower again even though there's no grass to be mowed.'

'Shit,' Bo muttered.

'Wow,' the cashier said. 'Meth, you think?'

'Oh, obviously, honey,' the Elderly Christy said. 'That family, I tell you what.'

'Gimme your keys,' Bo said. But she just snatched them off the table before Colt could say a thing. 'I'll be back.'

And then she was gone.

And it was just me and Colt and a whole lot of silence.

'I . . . I hope she's all right,' I said, finally, when the quiet was getting to me. 'Bo's mama, I mean.'

'Yeah,' he said. 'Well, I'm more worried about Bo. I'm glad she seems to stay at your place more than at her own these days.'

I just nodded.

And this time, after a few minutes of nobody talking, Colt was the one to break.

'Listen, I'm sorry I ain't called or—'

'I didn't expect you to,' I said.

'You didn't?' He sounded surprised.

I shook my head. 'No. I mean, when we . . . On New Year's, I knew you were leaving. I knew there wasn't gonna be a future for us.'

'And you're all right with that?'

'Yeah,' I said. 'Well, I mean . . . I don't feel bad about what happened, if that's what you're asking.' Then, after a pause, 'Do you . . . feel bad about it?'

'No,' he said, real quick. 'No, no. Not at all. That night was . . . It was great, Agnes. I just wish I'd been able to take you out on a date after . . . or before. I reckon you're supposed to do that before, but—'

'Colt, I really never expected you to—'

'But I wanted to,' he said. 'If I was sticking around longer, I would've.'

'Really?'

'Yeah. I like you, Agnes.'

'Oh.'

The surprise must've been written all over my face, because Colt said, 'You didn't know? I figured it was obvious. I always felt like I was staring at you . . .'

'Well . . . I'm blind, so . . . it's easy to miss that stuff.'

We both smiled and, for a minute, it was like that night in his trailer again, just the two of us, laughing through the awkward moments.

'Well, of course I like you. You're smart and nice, and a lot tougher than people realize, I think. I've liked you from day one. Not that it matters much,' he went on. 'Even if I was still in town, you don't wanna date a Dickinson.'

'That's not true,' I said.

'Well, you shouldn't wanna date a Dickinson.'

'I've done a lot of things I shouldn't over the past few months,' I said. 'And, honestly, I'm feeling pretty good about most of them, so . . .'

'Well . . . I'm glad,' he said. 'That you don't feel bad about what happened that night. And I am sorry I ain't called. Not because you expected me to, but because I wanted to. If . . . If I want to again, would it be OK if—'

'Call any time,' I said.

'All right. Thanks . . .' He let out a breath, like everything we'd just said had relieved a weight he'd been carrying for months. 'And, uh . . . I know you say we ain't got a future, but you know. If we're ever living in the same town again, maybe . . .'

That seemed unlikely. After getting out of Mursey, it was hard to imagine Colt or anybody ever wanting to move back. And even harder to imagine me being able to get out. But maybe that's what I needed – some hope, some promise of a future, even if it was unlikely. Maybe if I did what Bo and Colt and Christy had been telling me to, talk to my parents about how suffocated I felt, maybe it'd pay off. Maybe one day I'd get out of here.

'Maybe.'

BO

'We could hitchhike,' I say, watching as cars pull in and out of the gas station we're approaching. 'Shouldn't be too hard to get someone to stop.'

'Bo.'

'I mean, we gotta be careful because some folks are crazy, but—'

'Bo!'

Agnes yells and I flinch. I been yelled at a lot in my life, but it ain't never stung quite like this.

'Stop,' she says. 'Just stop. I told you – I'm leaving. I'm finding a pay phone and I'm calling my parents.'

'Agnes . . . please . . . Let me explain.'

'What were you gonna do, Bo?' She spins around to face me. We're in the parking lot now, standing beneath the Shell sign. She's looking off to my right, but I feel every bit of her anger. 'When we got to your dad's house, what were you gonna do? Break the news and then send me packing? Have my parents take me back to Mursey so I can rot there?'

'You don't understand.'

'I understand that I came with you – ran away from home, left my family, cut my hair off – because I didn't want to be left in that town without you. Because I didn't want to live without you. And you were just gonna throw me away! Make it all for nothing! Why'd you even bring me with you, Bo?'

'You wanted to!'

'But why'd you let me? Why'd you let me think this was about us?'

'Because I needed you!' I yell. 'Because I was scared to go alone!'

The echo ain't as loud here as on the back roads, but my voice still hollers back at us, faint but desperate. For a second, neither of us talk. A bald man pumping gas stops to look at us, but I try to ignore him.

'I needed you,' I say again, quieter this time. 'I couldn't tell you the truth because you wouldn't get it. You got folks who're always there. And I know those rules drive you crazy and they ain't always fair, but they're there. You ain't gotta wonder where they'll be every night or if they might get arrested or – worse – get themselves killed. You ain't never gone to bed scared. You want freedom, Agnes. I get it. But all I want is to go home.'

'I could've been your home!'

I swallow. 'Agnes . . .'

Agnes looks down, shakes her head. She's holding so tight to her cane that I think it might snap in two. 'You're a coward, Bo.'

'What'd you just say to me?' I demand.

'You—' She looks up again, and even though she ain't staring right at me, she's closer this time. Her eyes burning into my forehead. '—are a fucking coward.'

'Shut up,' I warn. I can feel that Dickinson coming out in me again. That meanness. That anger. 'Shut the fuck up.'

'No,' she says. 'You said I'm Loretta Lynn? Well, Loretta always says what she thinks, and here's what I think. You're so damn scared all the time. Scared of being alone. Scared of being hurt. So fucking scared you're all right with hurting other people. That's why you were never there when I woke up in the mornings. Because you gotta be the first one to leave. The first one to walk away. Well, that's too bad, because tonight, I'm walking away first.'

She turns around and walks toward the bright lights of the gas station's windows. I start to run after her,

246

but I trip and land hard on my hands and knees, scraping them all to hell. Utah's leash slips from my fingers, and, like everyone else, my dog leaves me.

She runs to Agnes, bumping her head against Agnes's thigh. Agnes stops walking and reaches down, groping for Utah's leash. Then the two of them start heading for the door.

'Agnes!' I yell, getting to my feet and picking my bag up off the pavement. 'Agnes! You ain't taking my dog, Agnes!'

She stops again. This time, though, she don't even look back. 'You don't even have food for her, Bo. And she hasn't had water all day.'

'Agnes . . . Agnes, please,' I try one last time. My voice breaks. Weak and hurt and . . .

Scared.

But she finds the door to the gas station and opens it. Utah looks back at me, like she's confused about why I ain't following. Then Agnes gives her leash a light tug and the two of them go inside. I can see Agnes through the windows. I watch her walk to the counter to ask about the pay phone. I watch the cashier point toward one on the other side of the store.

I've already turned around and started walking down the road, alone, before she gets to it, though.

Because I can't watch her dial the number. Can't watch her wait for her parents. Can't watch her leave.

Because she's right: I'm a coward.

AGNES

I turned seventeen on the day spring finally came to Mursey. For the first time in months, the grass didn't crunch beneath my feet. And in my jacket, I even felt just a little too warm.

'It's such a nice day,' Mama said as we climbed into the car that morning. 'And on your birthday. Couldn't be better timing.'

'Yeah,' I said. 'I'm getting tired of wearing gloves. Makes it hard to feel things, you know? And when you can't see, your hands are pretty much your eyes. Just another reason it sucks to be blind.'

'Yeah. It does, honey.' She said it real serious, even though I'd mostly been joking.

I'd gotten so used to talking like that with Bo – being honest but also making light of my disability – that I sometimes forgot that not everybody would respond the way she did. Most people in this town, and especially my parents, still saw my being blind as a tragedy. Something to be mourned.

Not Bo, though. She'd never pitied me. Not once. Not even on that day when she'd found me, lost in the woods. She didn't see me as someone she ought to feel sorry for. She just saw me.

Speaking of Bo . . .

'Hey, Mama, are you making my birthday dinner tonight?' I asked.

'Of course.' The car made a turn, and I knew we were only a minute or two from school. 'I was thinking some mashed potatoes, corn bread, and maybe fried chicken? Sound good?'

'Great. Can Bo come?'

I already knew the answer to this. Despite all my complaints about my parents, they'd really come around to Bo over the past few months. It had taken a while. Mama wasn't so keen on her after the trip to the river that had got me grounded. But now Bo was at our house almost every weekend, and she ate dinner with us more nights than she didn't. And if Bo wasn't around, they wanted to know where she was. Her presence was pretty much expected.

'Of course,' Mama said without even having to think

about it. 'I just assumed she'd be coming. Do you wanna invite Christy, too?'

'Um . . . Maybe another time. She and Bo don't really get along.'

'Oh. All right. Well, that's a shame.'

'Yeah. But . . . since Bo's coming over anyway,' I said, winding up for my real question, 'can I just ride the bus home with her?'

I felt dumb even asking. I'd gone to parties, drank beer, spent the night at a boy's house – not that Mama knew about those last two. But still. I was seventeen now, and I wasn't even allowed to ride the bus and walk home alone.

'Hmm.'

Hmm was a better start than an outright no.

'Bo can ride with me. That's her bus anyway. Then we can walk home together.'

'Well . . .' Mama paused. 'Is she good at guiding you?'

I had to hold back the groan I felt coming on. Mama had been the one to sign me up for mobility lessons as a kid. She'd seen me use my cane for most of my life. I didn't need to be guided all the time. Especially not in the middle of the afternoon, when my vision was best, on a route I walked every Sunday morning with her and Daddy.

Still, I gave her the answer that would get me what I wanted. 'Yeah. Real good. She's guided me lots of times.'

'Not on a busy road, though,' Mama said. Still, she gave in. 'Fine. Just be careful, OK?'

It was a small victory. And the prize was something I'd done before – just without her knowing. But still. Coming from my mama, this was progress. We'd been making it over time – slow, but steady. It was probably crazy, but I was starting to have hope that, one day, she and Daddy would treat me the same as Gracie. That I'd be allowed to do the same things she did, instead of having to sneak around and lie about it.

Maybe Christy and Colt and Bo were right. Maybe I did just need to talk to my parents and make them see my side.

I was looking forward to telling Bo the good news. And I didn't have to wait as long to see her as I'd expected.

During second period, there was a knock on the classroom door.

'Sorry to interrupt, Mrs Devore.'

My head jerked up, though I didn't have to see that halo of red and gold to know who was at the door.

'Do you need something, Bo?' my algebra teacher asked.

'Mr Martin sent me,' Bo said. 'He needs Agnes in the chemistry lab.'

'What for?'

'Ain't sure, ma'am. Said something about a test she took last week . . .'

Mrs Devore sighed. 'So he's gonna cut into my class time? That man drives me crazy. I really ought . . .' She trailed off, probably remembering she was in a room full of students. 'Never mind. Agnes, did you get the homework assignment down?'

'Yes, ma'am.'

'Then go. But ask Mr Martin to wait for his own class to talk to you next time.'

I grabbed my books, unfolded my cane, and followed Bo out into the hallway.

'I failed the test, didn't I?' I asked. 'I knew it. How does he expect me to do an essay about our lab experiments when I can't see half the stuff my partner's doing or the way the stuff reacts? And I've told him so many times—'

'Relax,' Bo said. 'Mr Martin didn't ask me to come get you.'

'He didn't?'

'No.'

I frowned at her as she led the way, turning down the hall that would take us to the cafeteria and the building's back entrance.

'Then what are we doing?'

She looked back at me, and she was close enough that I could see the big grin on her face. 'Celebrating.'

It was the first time I'd ever skipped class, and once the nervousness wore off, it was real exciting.

Bo had her mama's blue car, and we drove out to the river, to that same spot where I'd had my first beer and sang with Bo on the roof of the car. We hadn't been there in months. It had been too cold. But that day, it was warm enough for us to sit on the hood, our backs against the windshield, listening to the birds that had just returned from somewhere farther south.

'I got you something,' Bo said, hopping up onto the hood next to me. She told me to hold out my hand. I expected a beer, like last time, but instead she placed something small, round, and sweet-smelling in my hand.

A Little Debbie cake.

'Hold on,' she said, before I could say anything. 'I ain't done yet.'

Then she pulled a small, thin candle out of nowhere and lit it with a cigarette lighter. I couldn't help laughing.

'Happy birthday,' she said. 'I know it ain't much, but—'

'It's perfect,' I told her. 'Best birthday cake ever.'

'Liar. Blow out the damn candle.'

I did as I was told, then we split the snack cake between us.

'Tell me something I don't know about you,' Bo said, once we'd finished the Little Debbie.

'Uh . . .' But this game had gotten hard. It wasn't easy coming up with things Bo didn't know about me. I'd already told her so much. Told her more in the past few months than I'd told Christy in over a decade of friendship. 'Let me think about it. You go first.'

'All right.' She paused. 'You probably won't believe me.'

'I always believe you.'

'Well . . . I ain't never had sex.'

'Wait . . . what?' I sat up straight and turned to look at her. 'You've never . . . really? Not once?'

By now, I knew most of the rumours about Bo weren't true. Some had been exaggerated; others were just outright lies. But somehow, I'd never even questioned the idea that she'd slept with somebody. Probably a few somebodies. How could you get a reputation like hers otherwise?

'Not once,' Bo said. 'Too many people in my family get pregnant young and ruin their lives. I decided a long time ago I wouldn't be one of them.'

'Wow,' I said, stunned. 'I can't believe I lost my

virginity before Bo Dickinson.'

I clapped a hand over my mouth, mortified. Had I really just said that?

Now Bo sat up straight. 'What'd you just say?'

I felt my face start to heat up. 'I, um . . . I kinda slept with Colt.'

'You slept with Colt? My Colt? Colt Dickinson?'

'Um . . .' I pulled my knees up to my chest and leaned forward. 'Yeah . . . Since you went home, it was just me and him at his house on New Year's Eve and . . .'

'You had sex with Colt, and you didn't tell me?'

'I know, I'm sorry. I just thought . . . I thought you'd think I was lame, making a big deal out of sleeping with someone. I didn't want you to think I was dramatic or anything. Of course, if I'd known you were a virgin—'

'Don't make this about me,' she said. 'Shit. You really slept with Colt?'

I nodded. 'Is it . . . Is that weird for you? Since he's your cousin and all?'

'I mean . . . I reckon it's a little weird, but I really ain't that surprised.'

'You sure acted surprised.'

'I'm surprised you slept with him,' she said. 'But not surprised something happened between y'all. It's obvious he likes you.'

It's not like I didn't know this. Colt told me so himself. But it still made me smile a little.

'Wow. You slept with Colt . . . Well, I guess that's the something I didn't know about you.'

'Guess so . . . I'm still hung up on yours. You've really never slept with anybody?'

Bo snorted. 'Told you you wouldn't believe me.'

'No, no. I do. I'm just . . .'

'Don't get me wrong. I've done a lot of other stuff,' she said. 'I've fooled around with a lot of boys. Kissed even more boys. And a girl.'

'Whoa, whoa, whoa.' I threw up my hands. 'Forget the sex. What girl'd you kiss?'

She sounded embarrassed – and maybe for good reason – when she answered. 'Dana Hickman.'

'What? When?'

'New Year's. Seems that was a big night for both of us. Dana was the one who drove me home. I was upset and she was being nice and we made out in her car.'

'Wow,' I said. 'But you two aren't dating or anything, right?'

'No.' She sighed, and I could tell she was more than a little sad about that. 'Her daddy's a deacon at the church down on Peyton Street.'

She didn't have to say anything more than that.

257

'Poor Dana,' I said.

'Yeah.' Then, in this rush of words, like she was making herself ask even though she didn't want to, she said, 'How do you feel about me liking girls?'

I was caught so off guard that I just sat there, gaping, for a second.

'You've been nice about it,' she said. 'But we never really talk about it. And I know you go to church with your parents every Sunday and—'

'Bo,' I said, putting a hand on her arm. 'Honestly? At first, I . . . I was uncomfortable. I didn't say anything about it because I liked you, and I didn't want to push you away. But . . . the more time I've sorta sat with it . . . Yeah. My preacher has always said it's a sin to be with people of the same sex. But my parents always taught me that being a good person matters more than anything. And you're a good person.'

'Not everybody thinks so.'

'Well, they're wrong,' I said. 'You are. And you kissing a girl might be a sin, but me sleeping with a boy I'm not married to? That's definitely a sin. And the truth is, I don't regret that at all. So, the way I see it, I'm nobody to judge.'

'So . . . you're all right with it, then? Me being . . . bisexual, I guess? I ain't never used that word before, but . . . you're all right with it?'

'I think so. As long as you're OK with me fornicating with your cousin.'

She laughed and leaned back against the windshield again. 'Oh shit, Agnes. If people only knew. Slutty Bo Dickinson's a virgin who kisses girls, and sweet, innocent Agnes is fucking an older guy. A no-good Dickinson, to boot. I think I've about ruined you, Agnes Atwood.'

'No,' I said, sliding over and leaning my head on her shoulder. 'You've made me better.'

In a couple hours we'd have to drive the car back to Bo's trailer and walk to my house, pretending like we'd taken the bus. We'd have to go back to all the rules and the worries and the eyes watching us both.

But for that moment, on the hood of that car down by a dirty brown river, just Bo and me and nobody else—

For just that moment, everything was perfect.

BO

I walk along the shoulder of the road with my thumb out, both hoping and scared somebody'll stop for me.

It ain't until now that I think how dangerous this might be. I'm a girl. I'm alone. And I'm small. I can throw a good punch, and I've fought with girls twice my size. And maybe I kicked that jerk's ass last night, but he was scrawny. And drunk. And Agnes had helped some. There's no chance I'm a match for someone big and sober. Not alone.

But I can't think what other choice I got now.

I go maybe half a mile down the highway before somebody stops. It's a truck. A big eighteen-wheeler. And when it stops next to me, I try not to panic. The window rolls down, and I take a step back.

'Where you headed, honey?'

It's a woman's voice, though. Deep and raspy, but

definitely a woman. And I feel awful relieved.

I tell her Daddy's last known address. I got it memorized by now.

'I oughta be driving right through there,' she says. 'Get on in. You can help me stay awake.'

It takes an effort to climb up into the truck. My legs are too short. And after I try a couple times I feel a soft, wrinkled hand take hold of my arm.

'Come on,' the driver grunts as she helps pull me up.

Between the two of us, I finally manage.

And I see who's picking me up. She's small and old. With hair the colour of steel, pulled back into a bun. She's missing a few teeth, too, but she's got a nice, round face.

'I'm Pat,' she says, getting the truck rolling again. 'What's your name, honey?'

'Bo.'

'Bo,' she repeats. 'I like that. Why you out here alone, Bo? Where's your mama? You can't be more than fourteen or so, right?'

'Seventeen,' I say. 'Just small.'

'Still too young to be on the side of the highway in the middle of the night.'

'Yeah, well . . . that wasn't the plan.'

Pat asks a lot of questions. About Mama. About where

261

I'm headed. About why I'm alone. I don't say a whole lot, though. Just one- or two-word answers.

I'm still thinking about Agnes. About the things she said.

All of it was true. I just never thought she'd be the one to say it.

It ain't quite midnight when Pat says, 'We'll be there in a minute or two.'

I grab my stuff. She can't take me all the way to Daddy's house, but she can drop me on the highway. She even gives me directions, saying she's been in these parts before, and it ain't more than a five-minute walk to his front door.

I'm careful climbing out of the truck. And when I'm on the ground, Pat says one last thing.

'Good luck. And be safe, all right?'

'Yes, ma'am. Thanks for the ride.'

She drives off as I start walking the direction she pointed me. The little town is dark. Not too many streetlamps. And most of the windows in the houses and trailers I pass ain't got light in them. But I manage to find the tiny brick house with Daddy's address on the mailbox. And there's a lamp on in the front room.

I walk up to the doorstep and then just stand there.

It's late. And he might be in bed. Or he might not

even live here. Colt said his daddy ain't even heard from him in a while. I might be standing on somebody else's doorstep in the middle of the night. And I ain't sure how welcoming people are around here. This is Kentucky, after all. People got guns, and they use them.

At least in Mursey, they knew me. They might not like me, but they probably wouldn't shoot me.

In this town, at midnight, I'm a stranger.

I take a deep breath and knock anyway.

There are voices inside. But then the door opens. And I know the man in front of me. No mistaking him.

Red-gold hair.

Eyes the colour of sweet tea.

A couple scars from bar fights and brawls.

This ain't no stranger. But he's sure looking at me like I'm one.

'Hey, Daddy.'

He looks like he don't know me. Like he's never seen me before in his life.

'It's me, Daddy,' I say. I reach up and touch my hair. 'I know. With it cut this short I probably look like a boy, right? But it's me . . . It's Bo.'

'Bo,' he says. 'Bo . . . what're you doing here?'

'I came to see you.' Despite all the bad that's happened

tonight, I can't help smiling. 'God, I've sure missed you. Can I come in?'

'Uh – well, you see . . .'

'Wayne? Who's out there?' It's a woman's voice, coming from inside the house.

'Nobody!' Daddy yells, and I try not to take it personal. 'Listen, Bo—'

But I guess the woman didn't like Daddy's answer, because now she's standing behind him, looking over his shoulder at me. She's tall – taller than him – and with peroxide-blond hair. Except for the roots, which look about as dark as Agnes's hair. Her eyes are dark, too, and right now, they're narrowed. And even if her sight is as bad as Agnes's, there ain't no way she's gonna miss the resemblance between Daddy and me.

'Nobody, huh?' she says.

Daddy looks scared. 'Vera, this . . . this is Bo.'

'Hi,' I say. 'Nice to meet you.'

But Vera don't look like she feels the same. 'Bo?' She says it like a question and an accusation rolled up in one. And even though she's looking at Daddy now, he don't look back.

'How'd you get here?' he asks me. 'And where's your mama?'

'It's a real long story,' I tell him. 'But that's why I'm

264

here, actually.' And then, because I'm still out on the porch, I ask one more time, 'Can I come in?'

Vera looks like she wants to say no, but Daddy steps aside and lets me walk through the door, into the living room. There's an old beige sofa sitting against the wall, facing a little box TV. There are kids' toys all over the floor, too. Blocks and toy soldiers and even a teddy bear missing an eye.

'I'd better go check on Brent,' Vera says. 'Make sure the knocking didn't wake him up.'

When she's gone, I turn to Daddy. 'Who's Brent?'

'Our son.'

'I got a little brother?' I ask.

He don't answer. Just jumps right back into his questions. 'What's going on, Bo?'

'Right.' I sit down on the couch. 'Things have been real rough with Mama lately. She's been using a lot, and a few days ago—'

'Are you here asking for money?'

'What? No,' I say. 'Nothing like that.'

'Then why are you here?'

'Because . . . you're my dad,' I say. 'And right now I ain't got nowhere else to go, so . . .'

He blinks at me, like he's still confused. Just then, Vera comes back around the corner. And the crease

265

between her eyes says she's disappointed I ain't left yet. Which makes my next words even harder. So I keep my eyes on Daddy.

He used to rock me to sleep in his grandma's old rocking chair. Used to sing me Hank Williams songs when I was crying. Used to let me sit on his lap and watch the NASCAR race with him while he drank a beer. He's my daddy. And no matter what this woman thinks of me, I'm his baby girl. His family.

So I take a deep breath and spit it out.

'Well . . . I was sorta hoping I could live here. With you.'

AGNES

It wasn't long before the days started getting hot and the humidity made us all miserable. Farmers' kids stopped coming to school, pulled out by their parents to work in the tobacco fields. Summer was here, and we'd all be done with classes in a couple weeks. Then there were two and a half months of long, slow summer days to get through.

It got too hot to stay inside – Daddy refused to turn on the air conditioner until June to save money – so Bo and I started spending our afternoons in my backyard. We'd get off the bus at the church and head to my house. By the time we each poured ourselves a glass of sweet tea to cool down from the walk, Utah would be waiting outside for us, lying right by the back door. The first day she showed up, I nearly tripped over her. The second day, too, actually. But after a week or so,

I just expected to find her there.

There wasn't much to do outside besides get a sunburn, so Bo started bringing the book I bought her and making good on that promise to read some of the poems to me.

"'Hoodwink'd with faery fancy, all amort, save to St Agnes and her lambs unshorn . . .'"

Her voice curled around Keats's words, so slow and soft that I nearly drifted off. We were stretched out beneath Mama's dogwood tree, the only good shady spot in the yard. I was on my back, arms tucked behind my head. Bo was next to me, propped on her side as she read the long poem. Somewhere near my feet, I could hear Utah panting.

'What're we gonna do this summer?' I asked once she'd finished reading.

'What do you mean?' She was flipping through the book again, looking for another poem, one we hadn't read together yet.

'I mean . . . What are we gonna do? We can't just stick around here doing nothing for two months.'

'Well, I usually work the tobacco fields at the Scotts' farm to make a little money during the summer.'

I sighed. 'That sounds nice.'

'Not really. It's hot and exhausting, and you come

back covered in tobacco gum.'

'But it's something,' I said. 'Something to do. Mama and Daddy would never let me work tobacco. They'd tell me it'd be too hard with my vision and all. And maybe they'd be right. But I've spent every summer of my life stuck in the house, never leaving this yard.'

'I kinda like this yard,' Bo said, still turning pages.

'I wanna do something different,' I said. 'Something exciting.'

'There will probably be a few parties.'

Last year, that would have been all the excitement I needed. A couple parties, the promise of a few hours without my parents' eyes on me, that would have been enough. But now, it hardly did anything for me. Parties were over too fast, too similar to one another. And, at the end of the night, we were still stuck in Mursey.

'We ought to go out of town,' I said. 'Take a trip.'

Bo quit flipping the pages. 'You serious?'

'Maybe.'

'When I suggested that, we ended up fighting. You said I was crazy for even thinking—'

'I know, I know. But I been thinking about it, and maybe if we do it right, my parents will let me go.' I sat up so I could look at her better. 'I mean, they're letting me walk home from the bus stop with you, so that's progress, right? And the way I see it, my parents just wanna know where I am all the time. So if we plan it out right, give them all the details before we even hit the road . . . Maybe it would work?'

'You really think so?'

'Maybe . . . And we wouldn't be going far. I was thinking we could just go visit Colt for the weekend or something.'

Bo snorted. 'I see how it is. You just wanna go fuck my cousin again.'

'Shh!' I swatted at her. 'Keep your voice down.'

'Your mama's inside. She ain't gonna hear me.'

'There might be a window open. And if she got wind of what happened with Colt, she'd never let me out of the house . . . or she'd hunt him down and make him marry me.'

The second option didn't sound so bad, really. I'd never wanted to get married right out of high school, but if it meant moving in with Colt, getting out of here, I might've been on board.

And Bo could come, too. She could move into the guest room. Or sleep on the couch. I wasn't real sure how big Colt's place was. But we'd make it work. Maybe Bo could get a job singing somewhere in the city. There was a school for the blind there – maybe I could teach braille. Colt and me would be together, and Bo could find a boy of her own. Or maybe a girl. I could see her with a pretty brunette – a poet. Bo'd be great with a poet. The four of us would eat dinner together every night, then we'd sit out on the back deck counting fireflies and talking about the towns we'd escaped from . . .

'Maybe we could do that.' And for a second, I thought she was commenting on my fantasy. But then she added, 'We could go see Colt. Bet he'd like that, actually. And not just because you'd be fucking him.'

'Hush,' I said, blushing.

She laughed. 'All right. But really, what brought this on? You didn't even wanna talk to your parents about it when I had the idea.'

'I've just been thinking, and you and Colt were right.' And so was Christy. I hadn't told Bo about talking to her that day in January, and I hadn't talked to her since. But the things she'd said had stuck with me. 'Complaining about their rules won't change them. So, maybe if I just talk to them, reason with them, it'll make a difference. And, I mean, they let Gracie go to Florida with her friends for a whole week when she was seventeen,' I said. 'And Louisville's only a couple hours from here. Not near as far.'

'Your sister wasn't in Florida with a pair of Dickinsons, though,' Bo said.

'Stop it,' I told her. 'Mama and Daddy have really come around on you, you know. They like you, Bo. They don't care that you're a Dickinson.'

'Well, they're about the only ones.' She started flipping the pages of her book again. 'But all right. Let's do it. Let's go see Colt.'

'Yes!' I threw my fist in the air, the way Daddy did when UK won a ball game. Then I fell back into the grass, stretching my arms over my head. 'We gotta work out all the details. Starting with how we're getting there. Maybe Gracie will let us borrow her car?'

'We'll figure it out,' Bo said. 'Later, though. I ain't done reading yet. This poem's by Lord Byron. He's one of my favourites.'

I nodded and closed my eyes, sinking back into that pleasant place between waking and sleeping, more content and happy this time. Even as Bo's slow, sad words lingered in the sweltering air.

'"Thy vows are all broken, and light is thy fame: I hear thy name spoken, and share in its shame."'

'We could go in July,' I said. 'Maybe for the Fourth? Maybe there's good fireworks up there.'

'You can see fireworks?'

'Yeah. If they're bright enough.'

It was the last week of May. We'd been out of school a few days, and Bo had spent almost every night at my house. She'd leave in the morning and head to the Scotts' farm. They'd just started setting their crops, so she'd go help all day and come back to my house around dark, smelling like tobacco. She'd use our shower – always apologizing to my mama, like it was a huge inconvenience – then we'd head up to my room to watch TV and talk until bed.

Tonight – every night – we were talking about the trip to see Colt.

'Fourth of July's good,' she said. 'I get paid next week. Then I'll be helping in the field in June. I can have some money saved up for gas.'

That was still the problem, though. The car. There was no way Bo's mama would let us borrow the blue car for a few days to go out of town. Hell, there was no way that blue car could get us out of town. I wasn't sure how it got from one side of Mursey to the other without falling apart, based on how the engine wheezed and the frame clanked.

'How old do you have to be to rent a car?' I asked, picking up the brush from my nightstand and combing

273

through my hair.

'Older than seventeen,' Bo said. 'Don't worry. We'll think of something.'

'Well, we'd better. I'm gonna have to ask my parents soon.'

'Maybe we can take my aunt's car. Colt's mama don't leave the house much.'

I finished combing my hair and stood up, stepping over the blankets Bo sat on and walking toward the bedroom door. 'While we're in Louisville,' I said, shutting off the light, 'we ought to go to Churchill Downs. You know, where they run the derby?'

'I ain't watched the derby in years,' Bo said.

'Really?' I started making my way back to my bed. 'I watch every year. The whole family does. But I think Mama watches more to see all the hats the ladies are wearing in the audience. She don't care as much about the horses as Daddy and I do.'

'Well, we can go anywhere you want,' Bo said. 'How far's Mammoth Cave?'

'I don't know.' I climbed into bed, but I left the covers off. It was too hot, and even though Daddy had finally agreed to turn on the air-conditioning early, he kept it real low. 'I've never been.'

'I ain't, either. There was that school trip back in

274

seventh grade, but Mama couldn't afford it.'

'And my parents worried I'd get lost in the cave.'

'They really say that?'

'Sorta. They just kept telling me how dark it was and how hard it would be for me to keep up with everyone else.'

Bo thought about this for a moment. 'Well, we oughta go. Even if it's not real close. Ain't no way I'll let you get lost down there.'

I smiled. 'OK,' I said. 'We'll go to Mammoth Cave, then. And you ought to ask Colt if there's other stuff we should do while we're headed that way. Make the most of the trip, you know?'

'I'll call him this weekend,' she said.

'Great,' I said. 'Then we can make a schedule and get all the details lined up. And then I can talk to my parents and . . .' I was grinning so hard my cheeks hurt. 'Are we really doing this?'

'Sure seems like it,' she said.

I giggled and squealed quietly. 'This is gonna be great. The best summer ever.'

'We just gotta come up with something better next year,' Bo said.

She turned on the TV, the way she always did before we fell asleep, and found a rerun of *Bewitched* before turning it down just a little, just enough to hear the voices of Samantha and Darrin as they disagreed about how much magic Sam ought to be using around the house.

I dreamed Bo and I were walking down a dark path in a cave somewhere. Bo was holding my hand, leading the way as she held a lantern up for light. But when we reached the end of the path, we found a dead end. And when we turned back, the way we came was blocked.

As usual, when I woke up the next morning, Bo was already gone.

BO

They let me sleep on the couch, with an old quilt and a flat pillow Vera pulls out of a closet.

She don't say a word to me as she hands them over. But I say, 'Thank you, ma'am,' anyway. If this woman's gonna be my stepmother, I oughta be polite.

'See you in the morning,' Daddy says.

'Good night.'

They head off to their bedroom, and I set up camp on the couch. I lie there for a while, tossing and turning. I keep thinking of Agnes. Wondering how long she'll be waiting in the gas station for her parents. Wondering what she'll tell them about me. About the way I left her. I decide I'll call her tomorrow. And maybe, in a few weeks, she can come here. Once being mad wears off, she'll be happy for me.

I hope.

But I can't get all the things she said in that parking lot out of my head. Plus, the TV across the room is turned off, and I ain't sure if Daddy or Vera will be mad if I turn it on. So, in the silence, it's impossible to sleep.

I get up to look for the bathroom. I forgot to ask where it's at, but this house ain't real big. I head down the hallway, trying to be quiet so I don't wake up Daddy and Vera. But I find out pretty quick that they ain't sleeping yet.

'What am I supposed to say to her?'

Daddy's voice. Coming from behind the closed bedroom door. I don't wanna eavesdrop. Not the best foot to start off on. So I'm about to keep walking when I hear Vera, too.

'That ain't my problem, Wayne,' she says. 'I don't care what you gotta say – she ain't staying here.'

I freeze, my heart sinking down, down into my stomach.

'Vera—'

'I don't want her around Brent.'

'She ain't gonna hurt Brent. She's a good kid.'

'How do you know?' Vera demands. 'You ain't seen her in years. You didn't even tell me about her. The hell is wrong with you, Wayne?'

Daddy sighs. 'I thought her mama was taking care of it.'

It.

Not her. Not my daughter.

278

It.

'Well, she ain't. And neither am I, Wayne. This is my house. I pay the bills. I've been letting you freeload off me for six years. I ain't taking in nobody else.'

I wait. Wait for him to stand up for me. Wait for him to say I'm his kid. Wait through the long space of quiet for him to be my dad. Just like I've been waiting for years.

But it sounds like I'm gonna have to keep waiting.

'All right,' he says, sounding defeated. Not defeated enough, though. 'I'll do it in the morning. I'll get rid of her.'

The sun ain't even risen over the mountaintops when Daddy comes to talk to me the next morning.

I couldn't sleep. Not after what I heard. So I just been sitting here, staring out the window. Besides the smoky hills, surrounding the town like an army of shadows closing in, this place don't look too different from Mursey. Trailer homes, houses that look like they're about to fall apart, a church right down the road . . .

It's almost like I never left.

Like I did all that running and only ran myself in a circle.

'Bo,' Daddy says.

I look up from the window and see him standing there in his old T-shirt and boxers. He ain't even gonna get dressed for this.

'You're kicking me out, ain't you?'

He sighs. 'I'm sorry.' And the way he says it, like he means it, like he thinks it makes a difference at all, makes it so much worse.

'How come?'

He scratches the back of his head. 'I gotta think about my family, Bo. I gotta think about what's best for them.'

'But I *am* your family.'

He opens his mouth, about to answer that, then shuts it again. Swallows. 'Sorry.'

'Where am I supposed to go?' I ask. 'They'll put me in foster care, Daddy. Last time I went it was . . . it was so scary.' I didn't wanna start crying. Didn't wanna beg. But without warning, there are tears streaming down my face, and a tiny voice scrapes out of my throat, against my will. 'Please don't make me go.'

'Look, your mama and I had a deal.' He just sounds annoyed now, and it makes me cry even harder. 'She was gonna take care of you. That was what we agreed on. You living with me was never part of the deal.'

I wipe my eyes and take a few shaky breaths.

'Was you not paying a dime of child support part of that deal?' I ask.

He ignores me. Just like I expect him to.

'Brent's gonna wake up soon,' he says. 'If you're here, he's gonna have . . . There'll be questions, so . . .'

'So you want me to leave right now.'

He opens his mouth again, then shuts it. The man's got a lot of words he ain't saying, it seems. Instead, he just nods.

'Can I at least eat something first?' I ask. 'I ain't had nothing to eat since . . . night before last, I guess.'

He hesitates, like this might be asking too much. But then he sighs. 'There're Pop-Tarts in the cabinet over the stove.'

I almost say thank you out of habit, but I bite my tongue. I ain't thanking him. I ain't thanking him for nothing.

I find the Pop-Tarts in the kitchen. I also find an unopened bottle of bourbon sitting next to the fridge.

I ain't sure why the thought crosses my mind. But when I look back and see that Daddy ain't in the living room no more, I decide I'm taking that bourbon with me. I grab the bottle and my Pop-Tarts and run to the front door, where I left my bag last night. I shove the bottle into the bag and zip it up real fast.

When Daddy comes back down the hallway, I'm sitting on the couch, eating my breakfast.

He watches me until I finish. And when I finally stand up, he looks relieved.

I walk back to the door and sling my bag over my shoulder. I ain't gonna say goodbye.

I ain't gonna say goodbye, and I ain't gonna break down. Not again. Not for him.

My hand's on the doorknob when he says, 'Bo?'

I stop. And for a stupid, breathless second I think he'll ask me to stay. I think he'll realize how awful he's being. I think he'll say, 'Fuck Vera,' and put me first. I've been waiting so damn long for him to put me first.

But when I look back at him, he's holding his hand out. Handing me something.

Money.

'Just . . . in case you need it,' he says, giving me the hundred-dollar bill.

I look down at it, wadded up in my hand. A crumpled piece of paper that's supposed to make this better. To make him feel better about kicking his kid out the door.

'Don't . . . don't tell Vera, though,' he says. 'She don't know about this or the Christmas money I sent you growing up. She wouldn't like it too well.'

I look at him. At that nervous shake of his hand

as he scratches his head again. At the red in his cheeks. Agnes said I was a coward, and it seems like I get it honest. Because Wayne Dickinson is the biggest coward I ever met.

As I step out on the front porch, with the flimsy hundred dollars in my pocket, I suddenly think of all the poets we read. Of the writers behind those words I'd read aloud to Agnes and quiet to myself so many times. People who could turn pain into art.

I always wished I could do that. And especially right now.

I wish I could turn to my dad and say . . . something. Something beautiful and biting. Something that'll rock him. Make him feel this awful hurt I feel.

I wish I was a poet.

But I ain't never been real good with words. Ain't never been able to turn my own pain into nothing but tears and trouble.

And when I look back at him, with the door already closing on me, the only words I can manage sure as hell ain't poetry.

'Fuck you.'

AGNES

Colt's mama agreed to let Bo and me take her car – but only if we paid her a hundred dollars.

'Might only be by marriage, but she is a Dickinson,' Bo said after she told me the news. 'People in my family don't give nothing for free.'

Between my leftover birthday money and her tobacco money, we'd be able to pay for the car, though. Nothing was gonna get in the way of our trip.

Nothing. Except maybe my parents.

I decided to talk to them about the trip on Saturday night. It was one of those rare dinners where Bo didn't join us. She'd called to say she was tired after working in the fields. That was all right. I thought it might be easier to get my parents' permission on my own.

'Gracie says cheerleading tryouts end on Friday,' Mama was saying as she handed me a bowl of spaghetti.

'She says we can come pick her up in the afternoon.'

'Oh no. I'm gonna have to stay at the store that day,' Daddy said.

'That's all right. Agnes can come with me.'

I looked up from my dinner. 'Really?'

'Yeah,' Mama said. 'It'll be fun. You, me, and your sister can do a little shopping. Maybe get dinner.'

'And load all of Gracie's junk into the car again,' Daddy said. 'That'll be really fun.'

'Oh, stop. It won't be that bad.'

'That sounds great,' I said. And then, seeing my chance, I added, 'Speaking of going somewhere . . . I wanna talk to y'all about something.'

'What is it, sweetheart?' Daddy asked.

'Well, it's summer now, and without school, Bo and I have been talking about what we wanna do. And . . . we were thinking . . . about maybe going on a road trip.'

'A road trip.' The way Mama repeated it, with a low, flat voice, I knew we weren't off to a good start.

'Not a long one,' I said. 'Just over Fourth of July weekend. We wanna go see her cousin, Colt. He lives just outside Louisville. Just a couple hours from here.'

'We know where Louisville is,' Mama said.

'Well, he's got a job and an apartment there, and we wanna go see him. And a few other places, too. We already made up a schedule, so you'd always know where I am and—'

'I don't think so, honey,' Mama said. 'You want some garlic bread?'

'Wait – why not?'

'It's just not a good idea. Your daddy and I wouldn't be comfortable with it.'

'Is this because of Bo?' I asked. 'Because she's a Dickinson? You don't want me going somewhere with her?'

'Of course not,' Daddy said. 'You know we like Bo. It's not about her.'

'Then what?'

He sighed. Like this was already making him tired. 'Agnes.'

'But you let Gracie go to Florida when she was seventeen,' I argued. 'And that's a lot farther than Louisville.'

'Yes, but Gracie's friend's parents were with them,' Daddy said. 'There were adults there.'

'Colt's an adult.'

'He's also a teenage boy,' Daddy said. 'A teenage boy we don't know at all.'

'Gracie rode home for Christmas with boys you didn't know, though.'

'Gracie's nineteen now,' Mama said. 'She can make those decisions for herself.'

'Are you gonna let me make decisions when I'm nineteen?'

I didn't mean to raise my voice. Didn't mean to slam my fist down on the table so hard that our plates rattled. I'd been doing so good at keeping calm. At keeping my voice soft and careful. But just like that, my self-control snapped.

'Agnes.' Mama's voice was full of warning.

'I'm serious!' I shouted.

I didn't want to be shouting, honestly. But now that I'd started, I couldn't seem to stop. I could feel this going downhill. Could feel the walls closing in and the hope I'd clung to starting to fade. Maybe I was doomed to suffocate here, but I wasn't gonna go gentle.

So here I was, raging. Just like Dylan Thomas said.

'Because I have a hard time believing that when I'm nineteen, you'll let me make the same choices Gracie does. I'm seventeen, and you won't even let me walk home from the bus stop – right around the goddamn corner – unless Bo is with me. And even then, one of y'all is waiting for us at the door.'

'Watch your mouth, young lady,' Mama said. 'You're acting real ugly right now. We have rules for you because we want to keep you safe.'

'I can keep myself safe! I've been blind my whole life, not for five minutes. I know better than you what I can and can't do!'

'Where in the world is this coming from?' Mama asked.

'Everywhere!' I screamed. 'Everything is an ordeal with y'all. I can't walk out the door without answering twenty questions. I can barely get down the road, let alone leave this stupid town! And say what you want, but you treated Gracie different. And I'm sick of it! Sick of being trapped in this fucking house!'

'Enough!'

When Daddy's hand slammed down on the table, it was a lot louder than mine. Loud enough that I flinched and scooted back in my seat.

I was shaking. My hands and my knees and even my bottom lip. I almost never yelled at my parents before. And I'd definitely never cussed at them. Part of me felt triumphant, glad I'd raised my voice, glad I finally had one. The other part of me just felt scared.

'This conversation is over.' Daddy's voice was soft now. Dangerous. 'You're not going on a road trip with Bo. That's final.'

For a second, everything was quiet. No one moved.

No one spoke. And the silence hurt more than the yelling.

Finally, Mama let out a breath. 'OK. Well . . . Agnes, do you want some garlic bread?'

'I'm not hungry.' I pushed my chair back from the table, and the legs scraped the wood floor.

'Agnes . . .' Mama's voice sounded sad. And exhausted.

I turned in the kitchen doorway and looked back at the table. I couldn't see much. Just blurry figures where I knew my parents were seated. 'Tell me something,' I said. 'If I asked to go to Florida, like Gracie did, and there were gonna be adults there – would you let me go?'

They didn't answer.

Which was answer enough.

'Yeah. That's what I thought.'

I had a thousand memories of Gracie slamming her bedroom door. A thousand fights ending with a thud that shook the house and Gracie locking herself in her room for hours.

I learned from the best.

'Agnes!' Mama yelled from downstairs. 'If you break that door, I swear I'll—'

'You'll what?' I screamed, loud enough so she could hear me. 'Ground me? I'm already stuck here, so what does it matter?' I kicked the door, just to piss her off, but instead of hurting the wood, I hurt my foot.

I limped over to my bed, tears of pain and anger streaming down my face. I hated them. I hated Mursey. I hated this house and this little girl's bedroom I'd been trapped in for seventeen years. I grabbed a stuffed rabbit – Hopsy – off the shelf above my headboard and hurled it at the closet. It didn't make a sound, though. Just fell quietly to the carpet.

Frustrated, I started looking for something breakable.

'Agnes,' Daddy said, tapping on my door. 'Can I come in?'

'No!'

I heard the knob twist, but the door didn't budge. 'Agnes Atwood,' he said, voice firmer. 'Unlock the door.'

'Why? You wanna keep me locked up anyway. You got your wish. I'm not going nowhere.'

'Anywhere,' he corrected. 'Oh good Lord. I've been married to your mother too long. Come on, honey. Open up.'

'Fuck off.'

'Agnes!' he said, voice low. 'Don't you speak to me that way. What in the world has gotten into you? This isn't you.'

But he was wrong. This was me. I just wasn't the

daughter he'd known a few months ago. The daughter who'd never thought she'd get out of Mursey. The daughter whose biggest adventure was a walk in the woods behind her own house. That had all changed. Bo had given me a taste of real freedom. She'd helped me see how much I wanted it. She made me see how capable I was of surviving outside of this bubble, even when no one else thought I could.

And I'd been dumb enough to believe it was possible. To believe I could escape, even for a short time.

Daddy was wrong. This was me. It was just an angry, heartbroken me he'd never seen before.

There was nothing to smash in my room. Except maybe the TV, but that was too big, too hard to pick up. I curled in a ball on my bed, buried my face in my arms, and cried so hard that the back of my throat ached.

'Agnes . . .' Now it was Mama outside the door. 'Honey?'

But I didn't answer. Not then. Not the half dozen other times she and Daddy tried throughout the evening. I stayed quiet, shutting them out for shutting me in. Until, finally, it was past eleven.

'We're going to bed, honey,' she said. 'We'll see you in the morning, OK?'

I didn't answer.

'We love you, Agnes,' Daddy said. 'Just remember that, all right? We love you.'

BO

I wander the streets for a while, watching as people leave their houses and climb into their trucks. It's Wednesday morning, and for most people, the world's still spinning. Even if mine's falling apart.

I make a right turn. Then a left. I ain't sure where I'm going. Ain't sure what I'll do next. Until I end up in front of a run-down motel with a crooked sign on the front door. coal count r y inn it reads. It's the kinda place that ain't gonna care how old I am.

I give the hundred dollars to the man at the desk. He gives me some change and the key to room 5A.

It's small and dirty and grey. The carpet smells and the curtains got holes in them. I sit on the bed, hugging my bag to my chest. I ain't sure how long I sit there, just staring at the wall, listening to some people argue in the next room. But I sit and stare until my eyes feel dry and cracked.

When I take the bottle of bourbon out of my bag, it don't feel near as wrong as it should. I stare at the label for a long time. It's the same brand Daddy used to drink back in Mursey, before he left us. It's the same brand Uncle Jeff would get drunk on when me and Colt were younger. I've even seen Colt with a bottle just like this before. It's practically a Dickinson family tradition. Some kinda rite of passage. I put it off so long.

I've never taken a drink in my life. Not one. Because I didn't want to be like them. Because, other than Colt, every Dickinson I know has taken drinking too far. I wasn't gonna let that happen to me. I was gonna be better.

But when I take a swig, I know.

There ain't no way to fight destiny.

And this bottle, this gross motel, this lonely feeling – this is my destiny.

The first drink burns. The second's not so bad. And by the fourth or fifth, I don't feel a thing.

I turn on the black-and-white TV, watch an episode of M*A*S*H, and drink. I drink long. Drink fast. Drink it all. Until I pass out on top of the unwashed blankets.

I wake up with my stomach on fire.

At first I think I'm dying. I'm sweating and I'm panting

and I gotta run to the toilet. My vision is fuzzy, edges faded like an old photo, and my brain ain't moving right. When I trip over the empty bottle and have to crawl my way to the bathroom, I can't keep my head straight. Can't focus on what's going on. Why am I on the floor? Why am I dying?

I barely make it to the toilet bowl before I'm puking so hard it makes my whole body shake. And it just keeps on. And it hurts. And all I wanna do is sleep. And I'm clinging to the toilet for dear life, knowing if I don't, I'll fall onto the tiles and never be able to get back up.

This is my punishment. This is what I get for everything I done. I'm just like the rest of them. Just a lying, stealing drunk like my daddy and his daddy before him. I lied to Agnes, chased away one of the only people who's ever loved me back. And all I got for it was a hundred-dollar bill and a bottle of bourbon. Sounds about right for a Dickinson.

And then I'm crying. Sobbing between retching. I heard once the human body is made of seventy per cent water. But with all the crying and the puking and the sweating, I think there can't be none left in me.

When I think I can leave the toilet, I try to stand, but it ain't no use. My body's weak and empty, and all I can do is crawl. Drag myself back to the bedroom, to the phone by the nightstand.

Even with my head swimming and my vision full of black spots, I can still dial her number.

When she don't answer right away, I start to panic. Because I think I'm gonna die here. In this motel room. Alone.

And when she does answer, I start crying harder. Because I'm an awful person and I did awful things and I'm being punished and she ain't got no reason to answer the phone for me.

'Hello?' she says again. 'Is anyone there?'

'Agnes . . .' My throat burns and the words crack like snapping twigs. I gasp between sobs as I clutch the phone to my wet face. 'Agnes, I need you.'

AGNES

'Agnes?'

Bo's voice on the other end of the line almost made my heart stop beating. I'd never heard it sound so fragile.

But then, she'd never called me at two in the morning, either.

I was downstairs, my face still swollen from crying, when the phone had started to ring. I'd snuck out of my room, knowing my parents had long since gone to bed. No matter how angry I was, I still needed to eat, and I knew Mama would have saved the leftovers from dinner. I hadn't even opened up the fridge yet, though, when I heard the phone.

In all my life, I couldn't remember anyone ever calling our house in the middle of the night. For some reason, my mind immediately snapped to the horror movies Gracie made me watch when we were kids. Mama and

Daddy hated horror movies, but when Gracie babysat me, she always wanted to watch them, even though she knew they scared me. Even thinking of them just then, of the creepy calls girls always got in those movies, with heavy breathing and weird voices threatening them – well, it made me shiver and look over my shoulder.

Not that I could see if someone was behind me. I hadn't even bothered to turn on the lights when I came downstairs. I was regretting that now.

But then my thoughts shifted to worry. What if something was wrong? What if it was Gracie? What if something had happened to her? What if someone was calling in the middle of the night because the thing they were calling about couldn't wait until morning?

Another ring, and this time I moved toward the counter, using both hands to feel for the phone. It only took me a second to find it and answer.

'Hello?'

And that's when I heard her voice. The way it shook as she said my name. 'Agnes?'

That's when I really got scared.

'Bo? What's wrong? What's going on?'

'It's Mama,' she said. 'She got arrested.'

'What? How do you know?'

'Heard on the police scanner.' She sounded half out of

breath, like she was moving around her trailer as fast as she could. I heard rustling and the sound of a zipper.

'Bo? What're you doing?'

'They're gonna come here soon,' she said, the panic rising in her voice. 'I told you, Agnes. I ain't going back into foster care again. No fucking way.'

I felt like all the wind had been knocked out of me. Like I'd fallen and landed hard on my chest. Because I knew exactly what she was gonna say before I even asked the next question.

'What're you gonna do?'

She stopped. For a minute, I didn't hear any more rustling, no more movement on the other end of the line. Just Bo, trying to catch her breath before she said it.

'Run.'

BO

I know it must take the Atwoods hours to get to me. But everything after that phone call comes in flashes.

I'm lying on the floor with my face in the carpet, which smells like liquor and piss.

Then the door's opening and Agnes's daddy's picking me up like I'm just a sack of potatoes.

And then I'm lying in the backseat of their car, my head in Agnes's lap as she whispers, 'You're OK. It's gonna be OK. I'm right here.'

'Should we take her to the hospital?' Mrs Atwood sounds so far away, even though I can see her in the front seat.

'I don't think she's got insurance,' Mr Atwood says. His voice is coming from a distance, too. It's like I'm underwater, listening to the conversations happening on the shore. 'She's just drunk. She'll be all right in a little while.'

'That bottle was empty,' Mrs Atwood says. 'And she's so small . . .'

'Bo,' Agnes whispers, her fingers combing through my hair. 'What happened?'

It's too bright. I ain't never seen the sun so bright. I gotta shut my eyes, but I can still see it through my lids and I'm worried I might puke again, but I don't wanna do it in the Atwoods' car because they already hate me.

I have to push the words out. Because saying them makes them true. Makes the pain worse.

'He . . . didn't want me.'

The next time I wake up, I'm somewhere familiar. I'm on a camp-bed on Agnes's bedroom floor, one of her stuffed animals resting on the pillow beside me. Utah's there, too. Curled into a ball with her face pressed to my stomach. She ain't asleep, though. Her big brown eyes are wide open. Watching me.

'I'm sorry,' I whisper to her.

My throat's real dry and my head don't feel great, but the dying feeling has passed. Now all that's left is the guilt.

I hear voices down the hall. I figure they must be coming from Agnes's parents' bedroom.

'You can't call social services.' It's Agnes's voice, fierce and desperate. 'That's the whole reason she took off. They put her in foster care before and it was awful. You can't send her back there again.'

'We don't have a choice,' Mrs Atwood says.

'Let her stay here.'

'Agnes.'

'I'm serious. Why not?'

'For starters, it's probably best for you and Bo to get some distance,' Mrs Atwood says. 'Y'all aren't good for each other right now.'

'That's not true!'

'We just spent twenty of the last twenty-four hours driving back and forth across the state because you two decided to run off together,' Mr Atwood says. 'We filed police reports. Had to go get Gracie's car from a stranger's house, and worried ourselves sick. Sorry if we're not too keen on the idea of letting you two live under the same roof at the moment.'

'Damn it, Daddy. This is why I went!'

Both me and Utah jump. We still ain't used to the sound of Agnes yelling. I hope we never have to be.

'I made the choice to leave. Bo didn't make me.' She doesn't tell them I lied to her. And I'm glad. They hate me enough as it is. 'I didn't go just to joyride. I went

302

because she was scared and I couldn't let her go alone. And because . . . Because the idea of being stuck here, trapped here, without her makes me wanna die.'

'Agnes.'

'You think I'm being dramatic, but I'm not,' she says. 'Bo's the only good friend I ever had. Christy treated me like I was a burden. Like she was doing me a favour by being my friend. Bo never did that. And she doesn't pity me, either. She's the only one in this town who treats me like a real person. Like I'm not just some pathetic blind girl everyone's gotta take care of.'

'Oh, honey . . .'

'Stop!' she hollers. 'You're doing it now. You spend so much time worrying about me that you've made me feel trapped. Like I'm never gonna get out of this town. And Bo's the only thing here that makes it worth staying. And if you send her away, it's just gonna get bad again.'

There's quiet for a second. I reach up and hug the stuffed animal Agnes left for me. Squeeze the soft, fuzzy sheep toy to my chest. I'm proud of her for standing up for herself. Proud of her for being the Loretta I always knew she was. But I'm scared, too. Scared of what they'll say next.

'We talked about that,' Mr Atwood says. 'The night you left. After we argued. Your mama and I talked a lot about that. How we might treat you different from Gracie and . . . your future.'

'You did?'

'You sure didn't help your case taking off like that,' he says. 'Because now you're gonna be grounded until you're forty. But . . .'

'But?'

'But after that, we'll talk,' Mrs Atwood says. 'About the rules. About what's gonna happen after high school . . . We'll talk.'

I hear Agnes sigh, but then she says, 'OK. We'll talk . . . And what about Bo?'

My stomach churns, and I'm scared I'll be sick again. Utah turns her body some so she can lick my cheek.

'We know she's your best friend,' Mrs Atwood says. 'And we're glad she's been so good to you, but . . . honey, she can't stay here. Especially not with Gracie coming home this week. We don't have the space or the money.'

'And,' Mr Atwood adds, 'I still think y'all need some time apart.'

'But foster care—'

'There are some good people who are foster parents, too,' Mrs Atwood says. 'And . . . I promise, if we get wind someone is mistreating her, we'll do whatever we can to get her out of there. But for now . . . this is the best option, Agnes. I'm sorry.'

I turn my face into the pillow. It's over. I spent all this time running, all this time trying to escape, and it don't even matter. Because tomorrow someone from CPS will come and who knows where I'll end up.

'Can . . . can she at least come back to visit?' Agnes asks.

'Of course,' Mr Atwood says.

'After we're done with your punishment for this,' Mrs Atwood clarifies. 'Until then, no guests. None. And you're coming straight home after school this fall. No parties. No going anywhere without me or your father. You're on lockdown until we can trust you.'

'Yeah, I get it.' She pauses. 'I'm sorry. For scaring you. I really am.'

'Good,' Mrs Atwood says. 'An apology is a start.'

A few minutes later, the bedroom door opens and Agnes walks into her room. Her feet move quietly, stepping lightly over me, as she goes to her bed. The springs creak and she lets out a long sigh.

'Bo?' she whispers. 'You awake?'

But I close my eyes and keep still and pretend I'm asleep.

And after a while, when she's done been snoring for going on an hour, I don't got to pretend anymore.

* * *

I wake up early the next morning. Agnes is still sleeping, curled in a tight ball on her bed, snoring a little. Utah wakes up, though, and she follows me down the stairs.

Agnes's parents are in the kitchen. They stop talking when they see me.

'How're you feeling?' Mrs Atwood asks.

'Been better,' I say.

I look over at the door. My bags, the ones I'd taken on the road with me, are there. Waiting.

'We already called Child Protective Services,' Mr Atwood says. His voice is quiet, and I can hear the apology he ain't saying.

I nod. 'All right. When will they be here?'

'Any time now,' Mrs Atwood says. 'You want some breakfast while you wait?'

I shake my head. I don't got much of an appetite.

But I do have to say something.

'I'm sorry.'

They both look at me, surprised.

'I shouldn't have taken Agnes with me,' I say.

'The way she tells it, it was her choice,' Mr Atwood says.

'Yeah, but . . . I wanted her to.' I take a breath. 'I just want y'all to know I'm sorry. And I understand if you hate me.'

'We don't hate you, Bo,' Mrs Atwood says.

'We're not happy with what you girls did,' Mr Atwood adds. 'But . . . Agnes told us everything. About your mama and you looking for your dad . . . And . . .'

'And we're sorry, too,' Mrs Atwood says.

'Don't be,' I say. 'All the time I spent here with y'all and Agnes was . . . was about the only good memories I have in this town.'

They look at each other, and I know they ain't got a clue what to say to that.

A car pulls up out front. I can see it through the window. It's white and clean, and a tall, skinny woman in khakis climbs out of the driver's side.

'That must be the woman from CPS,' Mr Atwood says.

'Yeah.' My heart jumps into my throat, but I try to keep a straight face. I don't want them to know how scared I am.

The skinny woman knocks on the front door, and Agnes's folks go to answer it.

I crouch down and open my arms to Utah, who's sitting a couple feet away, watching me with those big brown eyes. 'Come here, you mutt.'

She runs over and starts licking my face. Even putting her paws on my shoulders, almost knocking me backward.

'All right, all right. Cut it out.'

She sits, tail still wagging, while she looks at me. Her mouth's open, like she's smiling. She ain't got a clue what's going on.

'I gotta go now,' I tell her. 'But you gotta stay here. I ain't sure when I'll see you again, but . . .'

I don't know when I started crying, but my face is real hot and wet now. Utah sits forward and licks the salt from my cheek.

'Quit it,' I say, but I don't stop her.

'Don't worry,' Mr Atwood says behind me. He's come back to the kitchen to get me now. I look at him over my shoulder, and he gives a soft smile. 'We'll take good care of her. I've actually always wanted a dog.'

'Well, you ain't gonna find one better than Utah.' I turn back to her. 'You hear that, girl? You're gonna be all right. But you gotta be good, OK?'

I wait, like she might answer. But of course she don't. She just keeps wagging and dog-smiling.

I give her one last scratch behind the ears and stand up. I have to wipe my eyes and take a deep, shaky breath before I follow Mr Atwood to the living room. Agnes's mama is in there, talking to the CPS lady, who looks over at me.

'You must be Bo.'

I nod.

'I'm Judy,' she says. 'I've picked a few things up from your house, but I see you have some stuff here, too. So that's good. Are you ready to go?'

I nod again. Because I know if I open my mouth to talk, I ain't gonna be able to hold in the sobs I feel trapped in my throat.

Judy picks up the bag by the door, and I start to follow her out.

'Wait,' Mrs Atwood says when I'm halfway out the door. 'Shouldn't we wake up Agnes? Don't you wanna say goodbye?'

But I shake my head. She and Mr Atwood look surprised.

But I can't do it. If saying goodbye to the dog has me this much of a mess, saying goodbye to Agnes might kill me. I swallow. Twice. And slowly, carefully, manage to squeeze a few words past the lump in my throat.

'Tell her . . . tell her I'm sorry, too. And I love her.'

Then I turn and follow Judy out the door, to her clean white car, putting Agnes's house behind me for the last time.

Just like always, I'm leaving before she even wakes up.

AGNES

'I'm coming with you.'

'Agnes—'

'I'm coming,' I insisted. 'I'll pack my stuff now. We can take Gracie's car. I know where my parents keep her keys.'

'Agnes . . .'

'That's why you called, isn't it? You know you can't just call and say you're leaving and expect me to stay here. What did you think I was gonna say?'

Bo didn't answer. Because she knew as well as I did that there was never a chance of me staying behind. If she'd wanted that, she would've called from the road, from a pay phone miles away, where I'd never find her. That was the only way I wouldn't follow her. She knew that, and she'd called anyway.

'Meet me behind the garage,' I said. I could feel my

pulse, like a drumbeat throbbing in my chest. It hurt. I clutched the phone with palms that were slick and shaky. I couldn't believe I was doing this. Couldn't believe what I was saying. 'I'll wait for you there. I'll grab some money, too, if I can.'

'But your parents—'

'I'm coming,' I said again. And this time, it was my voice that broke. 'I can't stay here without you, Bo. You're the only thing that makes life here bearable. My parents are never gonna let me leave Mursey, and if you go, I'll be trapped and miserable and alone. I'll die.' There were tears in my eyes, and I wiped them away with the back of my hand. 'Please. Take me with you.'

'OK,' she said. It sounded like she might be crying, too. 'I'll meet you behind the garage. Don't pack much. Just what you got to.'

'Got it.'

'And, Agnes . . .'

'Yeah?'

'Thank you.'

I took forty dollars from Mama's purse.

A hundred from Daddy's wallet.

And I had twenty-six of my own leftover birthday money.

I put on some jeans and tossed a few random T-shirts

into a bag. My cane was lying, folded up, on my desk, and I grabbed that, too. Then I headed downstairs, moving as fast as I could without falling. The house was dark, and I didn't bother turning on any lights. My shoes were by the front door, and I stepped into them just before putting my hand on the knob and—

I stopped.

I couldn't do this. I couldn't just leave in the middle of the night. The way my parents worried, they'd think something more sinister had happened. That I'd been kidnapped or murdered or something. I was so angry at them for the way they'd kept me caged. Furious that they treated me like a child. But I couldn't let them think I was out there dead somewhere.

I left my bag by the door and stumbled back to the kitchen. I flipped on the light over the counter and felt around for the notebook and black marker we always kept by the phone. It took a second, but then I felt the marker beneath my right hand.

With the paper in front of me, I realized I had no idea what to say. How do you tell your parents you're running away? That your best friend is in trouble, and you know if you don't go with her, you'll rot here, miserable and alone? How do you break your parents' hearts?

I didn't have time to think about it. Bo would be in

the backyard any second. So in large black letters, I wrote the first thing I could think of.

> *Mama and Daddy—*
> *I took the money and Gracie's car. Please don't worry about me, and don't call the police. I'm safe. But I had to go. I know you don't understand. I know you'll be mad. I'm sorry. But I have to do this. I love you.*
> *– Agnes*

I left the note on the counter, next to my cell phone, where I knew they'd find it in the morning. I could imagine their reactions already. Mama would yell. Daddy would go quiet. And I'd be long gone. But at least they'd know I was OK. At least I could give them that.

With my bag slung over my shoulder, and my cane unfolded in my hand, I walked out the front door for what I knew might be the last time for a long while.

It took me a few minutes to get to the backyard in the dark. My cane wasn't a whole lot of help in the high grass. Daddy hadn't mowed in a couple weeks, too busy with the store. But I finally managed, sliding my hand along the edge of the garage as a guide.

'Bo?' I whispered.

But there was no answer. She wasn't there yet.

I leaned against the garage, my heart pounding even though I'd been walking pretty slow. She'd be here soon. And then . . .

We'd run.

BO

'Hello?'

It's the first time I've heard her voice in months.

Five months, three weeks, and a day.

And hearing it now, on the other end of the line, has me damn near crying. I knew I'd missed her, but I had no idea how much until just now. And I realize it's a miracle the ache ain't killed me yet.

'Hello?' Agnes says again.

'Hey.' It comes out a croak. I swallow and try again. 'Hey . . . It's me. It's Bo.'

She gasps. The way you might if you saw a ghost.

And I'm the ghost.

'Can you talk?' I ask. 'If it's a bad time, I can—'

'Where are you?'

'Oh, um . . . Paducah. With my foster parents.'

'Foster parents,' she repeats.

'Yeah. Joe and Lucy.'

'I've been looking for you,' Agnes says. She sounds like she might cry, too. 'Me and Colt both have. We've been so worried. He's made calls, but we could never find out where . . . Are you OK?'

'I'm all right,' I say, even though the guilty feeling in my chest stirs. It's been there for a long time – since the night in June when me and Agnes took the car – and it's only gotten bigger, heavier over time. 'Joe and Lucy are nice. Kinda strict but . . . maybe that ain't a bad thing. It . . . it ain't nothing like before. The other place. The first time Mama . . . Well, it ain't like that.'

'Good.'

'Yeah. I really like Lucy. She's—'

'You didn't say goodbye.' She don't sound like she might cry anymore. Instead, she sounds mad.

I swallow, already feeling guilty. 'I know.'

'After everything we went through, everything I did . . . I woke up and you were just gone. I made my parents drive hours to go get you, even after you lied to me. You cried in my lap while you were drunk and sick, and I was scared to death. And then you disappear and I don't hear a goddamn word from you for months. What the hell, Bo?'

'I know. I'm . . . I'm sorry.'

I don't give her any kinda answer. I don't tell her why I ain't called, because truth is, I don't know. I've dialled her number a hundred times, but I always hung up before anyone answered.

When I first got here, after the CPS worker dropped me off . . . it was real bad. I was mad and hurt and scared. I cried at night. Yelled at Joe and Lucy during the day, even though they ain't never done nothing wrong to me. I even threatened to run away again.

I was a mess. And I didn't want Agnes knowing about it.

Then, come August, I started at a new school. A big school, where no one had heard of Bo Dickinson. I didn't have to think about Mursey or Mama or the trouble I'd caused. And as much as I missed Agnes – as many times as I'd heard a country song on the radio and got tears in my eyes because it was one we'd heard together, sang together – I knew calling her would open that door. It'd mean looking back at everything that had happened. And I wasn't ready for that yet.

I ain't even sure I'm ready now.

'Have you called Colt?' she asks. 'He's been worried sick, too.'

'No . . . not yet.'

'Well, you should.'

'I . . . I will.'

'God, I'm just . . .' She lets out a long, harsh breath. 'I'm so glad to hear from you, but I'm so mad at you right now, Bo. I thought you were my best friend—'

'I am,' I say.

'Really? Because first you lied to me, and then you left me.'

'I'm sorry,' I whisper. 'You called me a coward and you were right . . . but I'm calling now.'

There's a long stretch of quiet, and I'm starting to think I shouldn't have called at all. Not that I thought this would be easy, but . . . Fuck, I don't know what I thought.

'Well,' she says finally. 'Better late than never, I guess.' She don't sound happy, though.

I take a deep breath and try to get her talking about something else. 'So, um . . . how're you? How are things with your folks?'

'Fine,' she says, hard and cold. But then, with a relenting sigh, she softens. 'Better. It was bad at first. They didn't wanna let me go anywhere for a while. Guess I can't blame them for that. But we've been doing a lot of talking, and they're starting to ease up. They're actually letting me go visit Gracie at college after Thanksgiving.'

'Really?'

'Yeah. Just for a weekend. She's gonna show me the campus. And Daddy's driving me up to Louisville to look at U of L, too. Money's gonna be tight, but he says we'll do whatever we got to – take out loans, financial aid – he and Mama are gonna help me if I wanna go to college.'

'That's great.'

'We'll see what happens. I don't wanna get my hopes up just yet. And I still got nearly a year in Mursey to survive . . . but it helps knowing I might have something to look forward to.' She hesitates. 'And I might introduce Daddy to Colt while we're in Louisville.'

'Y'all are still talking?'

'Yeah . . . I haven't seen him since the summer, but he calls a lot.'

I know this is good news, but it hurts. Colt and Agnes, the two people I love most, have got each other now. They've got a whole world between them that I ain't a part of.

It's my own fault. I know that. I'm the one who ain't called. But still.

'He says your mama is gonna be in jail awhile. That she—'

'Don't got the money for bail? Yeah. I heard.' I take a breath. 'I think I'm kinda glad.'

I expect her to be surprised by this. Or hurt, maybe,

since it sorta means I'm glad to not be coming home. Back to her. But she don't say a thing.

'How's Utah?' I ask.

'She's all right. She sleeps on my bedroom floor every night. Right where your camp-bed used to be.' She laughs, and a weight lifts off my chest. I've missed that sound so damn much. 'I've tripped over that dog so many times getting out of bed. But Daddy loves her. He's got her trained to do all kinds of things now. Even taught her to fetch him a beer from the cooler.'

Just then, Lucy pokes her head into the kitchen, where I'm using the phone. 'Sorry to bother you,' she says. 'Quick question.'

I nod. 'Hold on, Agnes.' Then I look back at Lucy, and she smiles at me.

She's short, like me, but wide. In the last five months, I ain't never seen her wear anything but red lipstick and a white collared shirt that looks nice against her dark skin. She's got a good job at the newspaper, and Joe's a teacher at my school. They've got a nice house – small, but nice – and a little girl named Phoebe who thinks my name is Boat.

I asked her once why they'd want a foster kid, and Lucy said her parents had taken in foster kids. Over twenty. Some only for a night, others for years at a time.

And now, Lucy's best friend is a woman her parents had fostered. So she always knew she'd do what they did.

I'm their second foster kid. The first, Helen, is off at college now. Aged out of the system. But she still calls them every weekend.

'Sorry,' Lucy says again. 'Just wanted to check – you said Laurie's coming for Thanksgiving dinner, right?'

'Yeah,' I say. 'That still all right?'

'Of course. Phoebe and I are about to go shopping, and I just wanna be sure we get enough for everybody.' She looks at the clock on the wall over the stove. 'Don't be on the phone too much longer, OK?'

'Yes, ma'am.'

She gives me another smile, then ducks out of the kitchen.

On the phone, Agnes asks, 'Who's Laurie?'

'Uh . . . my friend. Or my girlfriend.'

'Oh!'

I can hear the smile in her voice, and I can't help picturing it. The way her blue eyes light up. The crinkles around them.

'That's great. Does she go to school with you?'

'Yeah. We met in English. But we ain't told anybody about us yet. Everyone just thinks we're friends. This place ain't as bad as Mursey but . . . I like her a lot. She writes real good poetry.'

'I knew it,' Agnes murmurs.

'Knew what?'

'Nothing,' she says. Then she goes quiet for a minute. 'I am happy for you, Bo. It sounds like you've got everything you wanted. Everything you were looking for.'

'Yeah . . . Except you.' I swallow. 'I miss you, Agnes. I'm sorry I didn't say goodbye.'

She don't say it's all right. Or that she understands. It probably ain't, and she probably don't. But she does say, 'I miss you, too.' And then, 'But I'm still here, you know. You can always come visit. My parents would like to see you.'

'Maybe.'

But I know I won't.

I'm glad she'd wanna see me again, after everything I've done. Mad as she is at me, she'd still let me in her house, which is more than I deserve. But going back to Mursey is the last thing I oughta be doing.

'And there's a college near there,' Agnes says. 'Murray. Maybe I can talk Daddy into taking me there, too. Maybe we could see each other. You could show me where you live.'

The thought makes me a little nervous. Bringing

Agnes here, bringing all the memories into my new world, is scary enough. But the idea of having her back for a day, maybe two, then watching her leave . . . I ain't sure I can handle it.

Not yet.

Hell, I already know hanging up this phone's gonna tear me apart.

She don't push, though, and I'm real glad for it.

'Hey,' she says. 'I know you gotta go soon, but . . . can you do something for me?'

'Sure,' I say. Because I owe her so much. I'd do almost anything. 'What?'

'Don't laugh, but . . . can you read me a poem? I don't even know if you still have that book I got you, but—'

'Give me a minute.'

I put the phone down on the counter and run to the little bedroom I share with Phoebe. The book is on my nightstand, next to my bed. I grab it and head back to the kitchen.

'I'm back,' I say, tucking the phone between my ear and my shoulder. 'What poem you want me to read?'

'You pick,' she says. 'One we haven't read before.'

I'd dog-eared half a dozen pages in the book by now. Poems that stood out to me. That I'd liked. I'd even marked up a few, circling lines and underlining whole stanzas. I find one of them. One of the poems I've marked all over.

I clear my throat and start reading Edgar Allan Poe's words, slow and careful. Agnes is quiet, listening. And for a minute, it's like we're back in her yard on a summer day. Just her and me.

I run my fingers across the second stanza and the four lines I've underlined there.

> I *was a child, and she was a child,*
> In *this kingdom by the sea,*
> But *we loved with a love that was more than love—*
> I *and my Annabel Lee—*

AGNES

'Agnes, you sure you wanna do this?'

We were sitting in my sister's car in the middle of the night, about to do what I'd been dreaming of for months: getting the hell out of Mursey. Being free. Being with her.

'No,' I said.

Because as much as I wanted to run, as many times as I told myself we'd make it work, that we'd come up with a plan . . . Deep down, I knew this might not end well. Stories like ours never did. But I remembered that poem in English, the Robert Frost poem Bo said was about how we tell our stories and change our histories.

And this was my story. This whole last year. And tonight. And wherever we went from here. This was the story I'd tell.

I looked over at her. Or, at the space where I guessed she was. It was too dark for me to see anything but a few dots of light on the dashboard. So I had no idea if I was looking at her face or not. Somehow, though, I felt like I was.

'But I'm doing it anyway.'

I heard her take a breath, then there was the sound of the garage door opening behind us.

Even though this story could end a thousand different ways, and even though chances were, it might not have a happy ending, it didn't matter. Because I already knew how I was gonna tell this story.

Bo Dickinson changed my life. She made it beautiful and messy. She made me happy, she scared me, she showed me I could be tough, and she showed me how it felt to live. She ruined my reputation and I loved every second of it.

Because she was the best friend I'd ever had. And I would have followed her off the edge of the earth if I had to.

That was our poetry. Our story. And it was one I'd be telling until the day I died.

'Love you, Bo,' I said.

'Love you, too.'

ACKNOWLEDGEMENTS

This book was truly a passion project for me – a book of my heart – and it would not have been possible without some wonderful, supportive people.

Thanks to my fabulous editor, Jody Corbett, who loves Bo and Agnes as much as I do and was crucial in crafting their story. Thanks as well to the whole Scholastic team – including Jennifer Abbots and David Levithan – who continue to make my dreams come true. My infinite gratitude also goes to the fantastic folks at New Leaf Literary – particularly Jaida Temperly and Joanna Volpe – for supporting my crazy ideas, even in their infancy. I am so lucky to have an amazing team on my side.

I have so much love for my own spectacular friends – Shana Hancock, Gaelyn Galbreath, Kate Lawson, Amy Lukavics, Laurie Devore, and Phoebe North. You ladies are the reason I want to write stories like these. Thank you for your love and constant inspiration.

Writing about Agnes's blindness was a challenge for me, despite having the same condition that she does. It takes a lot of courage to open up about your own disability sometimes, and I want to thank those who have encouraged me in this. The most thanks goes to my Disability in Kidlit teammates, Corinne Duyvis and Kayla Whaley. You two make me smarter and braver every day. And thanks to Holly Scott-Gardner for reading early chapters.

My mother would kill me if I didn't take a moment to thank my family, especially her and my dad, who never let me forget how proud they are of me. I know sometimes I act annoyed when you brag to strangers about my writing, but I'm so glad to have parents who support my work. I'm also lucky to have amazing siblings, grandparents, aunts, uncles, and cousins. Thank you all so much for everything you've done for me over the years.

And, finally – but most importantly – I want to thank you, my readers. Without you, I wouldn't be able to write the stories that I love. You give me the courage and the strength and the hope I need to keep writing. Thank you, thank you, thank you. You are my heroes.

ABOUT THE AUTHOR

Kody Keplinger was born and raised in a small Kentucky town. During her senior year of high school, she wrote her debut novel, *The DUFF*, which was a *New York Times* bestseller, a *USA Today* bestseller, a YALSA Top Ten Quick Pick for Reluctant Readers, and a *Romantic Times* Top Pick. It has since been adapted into a major motion picture. Kody is also the author of *Lying Out Loud*, a companion to *The DUFF*; *Shut Out*; and *A Midsummer's Nightmare*, as well as the middle-grade novel *The Swift Boys & Me*. Kody lives in New York City, where she teaches writing workshops and continues to write books for kids and teens. You can find more about her and her books at www.kodykeplinger.com.